SARINA BOWEN

MOO U

HeartEyes
Press

ONE

STICK WITH THE USUAL FAVORITES

Abbi

Thursday nights are always busy at Moo U's favorite bar and grill. By nine o'clock, I've been hustling burgers and wings for eight hours. But my apron pocket is full of tip money, so I can't really complain.

I have one party that just sat down, though—three women about my age wearing matching hockey jackets. "Welcome to The Biscuit in the Basket." I pull out my order pad. "The special salad tonight has spinach greens, apple slices, and a warm bacon vinaigrette. The special wings are Cranberry Almond."

"Did you say Cranberry Almond?" one of the girls asks, lifting one eyebrow as if she doesn't believe me.

"You heard correctly." I lean a little closer and whisper. "Nobody likes them. Stick with the usual favorites."

"Got it," she says with a smile. "I'd like a half dozen of the Honey Garlic wings, in a basket with fries."

"Wait—what are the flavors again?" one girl asks.

I could rattle them off in my sleep. "We've got Honey

Mustard, Honey Garlic, Tikka, Thai spiced, General Tso's, Chili Bacon, Chicken Parm, and—of course—Buffalo style in mild, hot, or wild."

And that's just the regular menu. The chef does a special flavor every week. Whiskey Maple is always a winner. Teriyaki is pretty good. But this week's special has been a disaster. Making a Thanksgiving-themed recipe was a nice idea, but I can't give away the Cranberry Almond wings. Not for love or money.

The other two girls make their choices, and I rush the order to the kitchen before it closes. Then I take up a position leaning against the nearly empty bar with my friend Carly, who's also on shift. She worked the bar tonight, while my section was in the dining room.

"We survived another one," she says, passing me one of the mints she keeps in her pocket. "What was your best tip of the night?"

"Depends how you look at it," I tell her. "A six-top tipped me fifty bucks. But my history professor tipped me fifteen bucks, and warned me to look over the Articles of Confederation before tomorrow's quiz."

"He gave you a *clue?*" Carly looks scandalized. "And a fat tip? I think he wants your body."

"Think again." I give her a smile. "He was here with his husband and their baby. I think he just felt bad that I was serving his dinner while the rest of my classmates are studying at the library."

And the man has a point. I work a lot of hours, and I go to school full time. There's no time for anything else. But that's just the way it is.

"Fine, fine. So he's not going to be your new boyfriend." Carly drops her voice. "Besides, I know you only have eyes for that crew over there."

My glance jumps involuntarily to table number seventeen. She's not wrong. Who wouldn't be interested in an entire table full of sizzling-hot hockey players? "I have no idea what you're talking about."

"Uh-huh," Carly says, eyeing them. Then she lets out a little sigh of yearning. "More for me then."

"You wish," I tease.

"You bet I do, Stoddard. Let's face it, table seventeen is the best thing about working here."

Once again, Carly is right. Neither of us can quit until springtime anyway. The owner pays a $1500 bonus to wait staff who work for him for an entire year. I need that money. So I'm going to smell faintly of chicken wings for the next several months, no matter what.

At least I can ogle the hockey players. Table seventeen is a long, high table surrounded by a dozen bar stools. And it's usually open by the time they wander in at eight o'clock, after practice. They're always starving for wings and fries.

For Carly and me, it's like a delicious buffet. The hockey team has as many flavors of hotness as The Biscuit in the Basket has flavors of wings. First you've got Tate Adler, who's six feet tall, at least. His flavor is what we'd call Brown-Haired Defenseman Hot. Next to him sits Lex, who's Pretty Boy Freshman Hot. And then Jonah—the Grumpy Hot Giant.

And we can't forget the Twins of Hotness—Paxton and Patrick Graham. I can't actually tell them apart unless I take their order. Paxton likes the Chicken Parm wings, while his brother goes for Buffalo style with extra blue cheese.

My favorite player of all, though, is Weston Griggs. He's a defenseman, sporting thick brown hair in a tidy cut. He has a winning smile and inquisitive blue eyes. But he's also got tattoos that poke out from the sleeves of his T-shirts.

I've had a thing for him ever since he scored Moo U's first

goal at the start of last season. And then my thing became a full-blown crush when he came into The Biscuit in the Basket that night and flashed me a huge smile, called me by name—or at least the name that's printed on my nametag—and then ordered a dozen wings and a side of coleslaw.

If I were a braver girl, I would have jotted my number onto his bill. But that's not how I roll. I'm the kind of girl who says nothing but then thinks about him all the time instead.

Weston often shows up in my daydreams. *Hey girl, I can't help noticing how sexy you look tonight. I have a weakness for women wearing T-shirts with hockey-playing chickens on them, shooting a Southern-style biscuit into a net. And even though I can have my pick of the campus women, I like mine wearing a polyester apron just like yours.*

I might as well fantasize, right? It's not like I have a real social life. I spend all my free time here.

Table seventeen has a big game tomorrow. So it's a little quiet over there. They're much rowdier on actual game nights. After a win, they drink beer by the pitcher. And after a loss, they also order shots.

But there are more wins than losses. Moo U is a hockey school, and our guys have brought home more league pennants than any other team in the Hockey East conference. And this year could be big. The team looks great. They could go all the way to the Frozen Four.

They're decent tippers, too. Especially for college boys.

"Tell you what," Carly says. "All my other tables are gone. And since you can't stop watching the hockey players, how about you tip me forty bucks and you can close 'em out in my place? You know you want to."

"Forty bucks?" I yelp. "They're not drinking tonight. I'll be lucky to break even on that deal."

"But I'm giving you my eye candy! Duh. And besides—

they just ordered two pitchers of beer. It's someone's birthday." Carly chirps. "Weston's I think."

"Weston's birthday," I say stupidly.

"Yup!" She holds out her hand. "Now pass me forty bucks, and bring the tattooed hottie his birthday beer. You know you want to," she repeats.

My glance travels, unbidden, to the strapping defenseman at the head of the table. The one whose smile makes my heart go pitter-patter. And now I know when his birthday falls. That will come in handy when we're married.

"Earth to Abbi! Are you going to let me go off shift, or what?"

"Fine," I say, digging two twenties out of my apron and passing them to her. "Go already."

"Give Weston my love," she says with a smirk. "Along with the big moony eyes you always give him."

"I don't give anyone moony eyes."

"Just keep telling yourself that." She winks, tosses her ponytail, and leaves for the night.

Weston must be turning twenty-one, or maybe twenty-two, if he played junior hockey before college. I'm surprised he's celebrating his birthday so quietly with his teammates. It's not unusual for Weston to show up here with a girl on his arm. Or on his knee. Or anywhere on his person, really.

It's a different girl every time. He's a player in every sense of the word. The women always seem happy to be his girl of the hour, though. There's always a lot of giggling at table seventeen when Weston has female company.

He likes them giggly. That's his type, I guess.

I really have no chance at all.

The bartender wakes me from this daydream by setting two pitchers on the bar, then knocking his knuckles against the wood. Twice. "Carly around?" he calls to me.

"I've got it," I say, darting over to load the beer onto a tray. I carry the pitchers and a stack of glasses to table seventeen.

There are two freshmen at the table who probably aren't twenty-one yet. But Kippy, the lazy manager, left a half hour ago, and these guys all walk home. I'm not in the mood to play cop, so everyone gets a glass.

"Evening boys," I say, setting the pitchers down in front of Weston one at a time. "This one is the IPA, and this one is the IPL. Enjoy. Does anyone need anything else?"

"Yeah we do!" one of the freshmen shouts. "You know it's Weston's birthday? Maybe you should do a striptease for us."

Oh lovely. I don't know this jerk's name, but I make a mental note to remember his face, so I can stay well clear of his hands. There's enough trouble in my life already.

"Rookie!" Weston barks. "Our server doesn't need a side of sexual harassment with her job description tonight. Don't be that kind of asshole. And only an idiot would be rude to the woman who serves your food at least three nights a week."

I let out a startled laugh, and fall a little more deeply in love with Weston. "What an *excellent* point."

But he isn't done. "Now put ten bucks in the kitty." He pats the table and waits.

The freshman blinks. But then he reaches for his wallet. The team kitty is a stash of money that builds all season long. The captain and assistant captains are in charge of deciding which infractions require a contribution. And in the spring—after the last game is played—they choose a charity and make a gift.

Weston puts the younger man's ten into an envelope in his backpack. "Now apologize to Gail," he demands. "Or I'm not pouring you one of my birthday beers."

The younger guy scowls. "Sorry, Gail," he says gruffly. "My bad."

Weston turns his handsome face toward mine and meets

my gaze. His is warm and cautiously amused. "How would you grade that apology?"

"Um...?" I've gotten a little lost in his blue eyes. "Sorry?"

"I think the kid deserves no better than a B-. But I'll leave it up to you. Should we let him pass?"

"Sure," I say, not wanting to make a fuss. "I've heard far worse, to be honest." And I wish I could say it was rare.

"That is unfortunate," he says softly. "But not tonight, okay? It's my job to train up the rookies—for the good of Moo U, and for the good of hockey. It's my sacred, noble mission."

"Sure it is." His buddy Tate elbows him. "Last night you said that convincing me to order the Thai wings was your sacred, noble mission."

Weston shrugs. "A guy can have two sacred, noble missions."

"Especially on his birthday," I add. "Cheers, boys. Drink up, because it's last call." We close at ten on weeknights.

Then I leave them to it. I need to do some side work so I can leave as soon as they're through.

By the time I deliver the sorority girls' food, the candles on the tables are burning low in their votive cups. This is my favorite time of night at The Biscuit in the Basket. It's peaceful, as the murmur of quiet conversation replaces the dull roar we hear throughout the dinner rush.

The Biscuit has a cozy, old-time feel, like it's been here forever. The walls are paneled in dark brown wood, but most of the space has been given over to group photos of Moo U sports teams from every consecutive year since the turn of the last century.

I love to stop for a glance at the oldest photos, with the baseball players in their baggy, pinstriped knickers. And the hockey players with their 1960s haircuts. The women's team photos start up a bit later, in the eighties. There's basketball and cross country too.

One thing you won't find on these walls, though, is a photo of a football team. Moo U doesn't have one. We're a D1 hockey school, and we do well in lacrosse and baseball, as well as winter sports like skiing and ski jumping. But football just isn't very Vermonty. So we don't bother.

To finish up the night's work, I take a seat at an empty table and roll silverware for tomorrow's shift. And I just happen to pick a table that's within earshot of table seventeen. Eavesdropping is good service, right? I'm easy to find if they need anything.

Plus, it's entertaining. The hockey players are making celebratory toasts. "To winning the league this year!" one of the twins says.

"The *league*?" Weston yelps. "Why not the national championship? Aim high, Patrick."

"To Professor Reynolds for postponing the Rocks for Jocks test!"

"Wait, really? It was postponed?"

"To cold beer and warm women!"

That was the obnoxious freshman again. Weston ignores him this time.

"To Weston!" Tate cheers. "Another trip around the sun!"

"Aw, shucks, guys. You're all buying me dinner, right?" He sets down his beer. "Speaking of dinner, I almost forgot about my flyers." He pulls his backpack off the floor and unzips it. He pulls out a folder from the copy shop and flips it open. "It's time to hang up my sign."

Tate looks over his shoulder and laughs. "No *way*. You're doing that again? Why?"

"Because I love Thanksgiving. It's my favorite holiday."

"You could come out to our farm, you know," Tate argues. "You have a standing invitation."

"That is a tempting offer, especially because your grandma makes that apple pecan tart with the crinkly edges." Weston makes a motion with his fingers, as if crinkling imaginary dough. "And the crumble topping is spectacular."

It's so cute I find myself smiling into the silverware bin.

"So what's the problem, then?" Tate demands. "And if you pick on my grandma's cooking, I will hurt you."

"Your grandmother's cooking is awesome. My problem is with your father's football picks. I can't root for the Patriots, man. Besides, this way I'm providing a public service."

"What service?" Someone snatches a flyer out of the folder and reads it aloud. *"Rent a boyfriend for the holiday. For $25, I will be your Thanksgiving date. I will talk hockey with your dad. I will bring your mother flowers. I will be polite, and wear a nicely ironed shirt. Note: I don't cook, so I am not able to bring a dish. I'm from out of town, and have no plans for the holiday. But I love Thanksgiving, and would be happy to celebrate with you. Especially if your mother is a good cook. Or your father. I'm not sexist."*

There's a smattering of laughter and sarcastic applause.

"You're charging money?" one of the freshmen squeaks.

"It's a nominal fee," Weston says with a shrug.

"But it makes you sound desperate," the youngster says.

"Nah, it makes me sound like I value my own time and company. And I always get multiple offers. The fee keeps the nutters away. Only women who really need my help will apply."

Someone asks: "What if it's a dude who calls?" And the whole table snickers.

I'm surprised when Weston just shrugs. "That would be fine I guess. Fake love is fake love."

Twelve hockey players howl with laughter.

And I am captivated. There's nothing on Netflix that's half as interesting as Weston Griggs hiring himself out on Thanksgiving. *Boyfriend for Rent.*

I wonder if there's a rent-to-own option?

"Weston, is this even legal?" one of the twins asks. "Coach will be pretty pissed if you're busted for solicitation."

"Does the team have a bail fund?" his brother asks. And then they high-five each other.

"Don't twist my good deed into something tawdry." Weston lifts his perfect, masculine jaw and gives the twins a glare. "My intentions are pure. Last Thanksgiving I had a lovely meal with a sophomore nursing student in Winooski. She'd recently broken up with her high school boyfriend, and her parents were upset about the breakup. God knows why. So I went along and they didn't mention him once the whole day."

"Huh," Tate says. "So I guess she got her twenty-five bucks' worth in peace of mind."

"Exactly. And I enjoyed a lovely turkey—cooked sous vide style, so it was extra moist and juicy. Then her mother rubbed the skin with butter and crisped it up under the broiler. And there was a sausage stuffing with water chestnuts so good I almost cried."

"Water chestnuts?" Tate shudders. "That's just wrong."

"No, it's glorious." Weston puts down his beer glass. "And now I'm hungry again. We've got to stop talking about Thanksgiving. It's a whole week away."

"You started it," Tate says with a chuckle. "And the Pats are totally going to win this year."

"Bullshit," Weston mutters. "Maybe I should come over just so I can watch your dad cry."

"Bet you a four-pack of Goldenpour they win," Tate challenges.

"Deal. We'll settle up after the holiday."

Then Weston gets up and hangs his flyer on the bulletin board right by the door.

They depart forty minutes later, leaving behind a tip of fifty-five bucks. Totally worth it! I yawn my way through the rest of my side work until it's time to race home to burn the midnight oil for my test.

But before I leave the Biscuit for the night, I stop in front of the bulletin board. If I hadn't overheard that conversation tonight, I wouldn't have looked twice at this sign. Weston didn't put his name on it. There's nothing there to advertise the fact that whoever hires Weston on Thanksgiving is getting a date with the hunkiest man on the hockey team.

I reach out and tear one of the phone numbers off the bottom corner. And then I tuck it into my pocket on my way out the door.

TWO
PEOPLE GET RESTLESS

Weston

My phone rings when I'm on the way into my econ class. This class bores me, so I stop outside the lecture hall and answer my brother's call. "What's shakin', Stevie?"

"You're coming home for Thanksgiving, right?"

Uh-oh. Cue the awkward silence. "Nah, I'm sorry. My practice schedule is awfully tight."

"Bullshit!" he says immediately. "You're a lying liar who lies!"

"Aw, come on now. It doesn't make sense for me to rent a car and drive across the state for a meal, Stevie. I'm a busy guy, and it will be a—"

"Shit show," he grumbles. "That's why you should feel obligated to come home and suffer with me. It's not like we live in Texas, asshole. Get a Zipcar. Drive a hundred miles. A hockey game is longer than your drive home."

"I can't, man. I have a date." This is strictly true, seeing as I have at least three offers already this morning.

12

"A date," he says, his voice betraying flat disbelief. "On Thanksgiving."

"Yup."

"That's what you said last year, too."

"It was true last year as well." He doesn't need to know that I've hired myself out. In truth, I feel bad that Stevie has to suffer through Thanksgiving at one of our parents' homes. He's a year behind me at Dartmouth, which is just a few miles away from our mom's house in Norwich and a few more miles from our dad's place in Fairlee. He can't blame the hockey schedule, either, because he hasn't played since high school.

He's trapped. But that is not my fault. "You'll have Lauren's company though, right?" Our sister lives in town with her fiancé.

Stevie makes a disgusted sound. "You know what she's like right now. All she can talk about is the wedding. Flowers and colors and the rest of that bullshit."

We both shudder. As the owner of a dick, weddings were never interesting to me. But since our parents' spectacular divorce a couple of years ago, just the *idea* of marriage makes me feel a little squicky.

At some point in the near future, I'm going to have to put on a tux and watch my sister marry her boyfriend of three years. I'm going to have to clap and smile and try not to suffocate in my bow tie, while I watch my sister make the biggest mistake of her life.

Nothing against her guy, either. He seems nice enough for now. That's the problem, though. Once the glow wears off, people get restless. And then they do stupid, crazy things to each other. And they make their kids watch.

Fun times.

"Look." I level with my brother. "I'm not coming home for

Thanksgiving. You don't have to either, you know. You don't owe it to them."

"Dad, though. He'll be all alone."

"That's true," I murmur. And I feel for the guy. "But our father is an adult, you know? The destruction of his marriage is about to celebrate its third anniversary. He can either stew about it, or he can find a way to move on."

"Good luck telling him that."

"Oh I've tried." I was gentle, of course. I'm not a monster. The problem is that my father prefers rage to action. He'll spend the whole holiday muttering about "that bitch," which is how he refers to our mother.

Or, if Stevie went to Mom's house instead, Dad would be mad at him for days. You really can't win with him anymore.

He doesn't see how much this upsets us either. Sure, we were all pretty astonished when Mom left Dad. It was brutal. But she's still our Mom, and she still loves us. Three years later, and our father still expects us to take sides. It's fucking exhausting.

I shove a hand into my pocket and absently rub the smooth piece of obsidian stone that's resting there. Our assistant coach is really into crystals. He said obsidian would help me get rid of "emotional blockage" and give me strength, clarity, and compassion.

But what if I'm not the one who needs it? How much obsidian can I sneak into my father's house without him noticing?

My parents' divorce is why I no longer go home for Thanksgiving. And also why I will never *ever* fall in love. It turns you into a bitter freak when it ends.

"Dude, you *have* to come home for Christmas," my brother says. "If you tell me you have a date, I'm going to drive up there and haul you back here myself."

"Yeah, okay." There's no way I can pretend to be busy on Christmas Day. "I'll come home. We'll stay with Dad, yeah?"

"Yeah. And bring some nice clothes."

"Why?" I demand. "For church?" My parents still insist on attending the same church. Neither one of them is willing to be the one who leaves. As far as I can tell, they sit on opposite sides of the room shooting daggers at each other while the priest stands up front preaching about love and forgiveness.

"Worse," Stevie grumbles. "Mom is throwing an engagement party for Lauren on the day before Christmas Eve."

"Oh shit," I whisper. Then I let out a groan.

"Yeah." My brother sighs. We both know what that means —Mom and Dad at the same party for the first time in three years. With alcohol, too. It could be bad bad *bad*. "You'll be there, right? If you try to blow this off, I'll tell Dad it was you who scratched his Mercedes by having sex up against it."

"*Rude*," I grunt. "You know that was a freak accident." I'd set my date up on the hood and we'd had a fine time. Who could have guessed that her short little skirt had metal grommets on the back? What kind of fashion designer thought that was a good idea?

"Still your fault, though." He snickers. "Don't make me do it. If I have to go to this thing, then so do you."

"Yeah, okay," I grumble. It's not my sister's fault that our family has become just like a daytime TV show. If she's crazy enough to get engaged, I'll make sure there's someone at her party who isn't going to make a scene.

Even if it hurts me. And I expect it to hurt plenty.

"Who's this date with, anyway?" my brother asks.

"Hmm?"

"Your date. On Thanksgiving."

"Oh, uh, a new girl." I haven't chosen one yet, of course.

"They're all new girls with you."

15

"You say that like it's a bad thing."

He snorts. "Yeah. But we're not all hockey stars. The talent pool works harder for you than it does for us mere mortals, bro."

"It's good work if you can get it." Just because I'm never marrying a woman doesn't mean that I don't enjoy them.

"Later, Weston."

"Later, punk."

I slip into the back of the lecture hall and nab an empty seat. I'm just settling in to the lecture when my phone buzzes with a text. I don't look right away, because I assume it's Stevie busting on me again. He probably thinks he can guilt me into coming home for Thanksgiving.

But as the professor drones on about monetary policy, I decide to check. I don't want to be a dick, but it's a big lecture hall and I've perfected the art of texting while pretending to pay attention.

The number is unfamiliar. It must be another inquiry for Thanksgiving. I've gotten three already this morning.

Hi there, the new one begins. *My name is Abbi. I saw your sign at the Biscuit, and I wonder if I could take you up on your Boyfriend Rental offer. I'm a junior here at Moo U, and my family's place is just fifteen miles away in Shelburne.*

Hmm. Two of the other inquiries are from girls who live further afield. So I already like Abbi. I'm just about to respond when an additional message appears.

She adds: *You should also know that my step-stepmother is the sort of cook who goes to a lot of trouble. There will be a dozen homemade dishes on the table. Like butternut squash soup with shredded bacon and croutons on top. Roasted turkey, of course. But also steamed Chinese dumplings filled with turkey and scallions. Plus an army of side dishes, and three kinds of pie. She's a superstar cook.*

Well, damn. My mouth is watering already. And before I think better of it, I ask a follow-up question. *Is there a dipping sauce with the dumplings? Wait, was that a rude opener? Let me try again. Hi Abbi! I'm Weston. I really like Thanksgiving, and your dumplings intrigue me.*

Abbi: *Your curiosity is justified. You can't go home with just anyone for Thanksgiving, right? What if the mashed potatoes were out of a box?*

Weston: *Bite your tongue! Only a monster would make boxed mashed on Thanksgiving.*

Abbi: *I'm just pointing out that you have to be careful going home with strangers. And, for the record, last year there were two different dipping sauces for the dumplings. There was soy ginger and also cranberry.*

That does sound promising. I think Abbi's Thanksgiving spread sounds like a winner. I decide to just accept it on the spot, and let the other women down gently.

Weston: *Okay Abbi, you're on. Please text the details when you're ready. I'm happy to meet you anywhere on campus. I don't have a car though.*

Abbi: *I can drive. And I really appreciate this. Holidays can be tense.*

Weston: *True Story. Send me the deets and I'll see you on Thursday.*

When Thanksgiving Day arrives, I am careful to arrive—showered and shaven—at Abbi's front door right on time. I might even be a minute or two early. I'm wearing a crisp Dad-pleasing shirt and my best Mom-pleasing tie, because I make it a point to always know my audience.

I get teased for it, too. The guys at the hockey house call me

Mr. Smooth.

"You're referring to my skating, right?" I'd said the first time I heard it.

"Nah, man. Everything about you is smooth. The hair. The whole polite-guy thing. The ladies really go for it. I bet even your ass is smooth, but I don't need any proof, thanks." That had gotten a lot of laughs.

So sue me. Life is easier when you take control of every situation. If my skills with hair products and parents earn me the occasional ribbing, I'm perfectly okay with that.

Abbi's address turns out to be an old Victorian mansion that's been chopped up into smaller apartments. In the wallpapered vestibule, I push the buzzer for apartment 2, and a female voice calls, "Just a second!" on the other side of the door.

I wonder what Abbi is like. It doesn't matter very much, of course. I haven't agreed to marry her. It's just one day of my life. And people fascinate me, so even if Abbi's family is irritating as fuck, I probably won't take it personally.

But I have a good feeling about Abbi herself. She's local, which is interesting. Vermonters are pretty cool. They have a rugged mentality, and they rarely complain. And they're usually hockey fans. What's not to like about that?

The door opens, and I immediately lose my train of thought. I'm blinking at a pretty blond woman with shoulder-length hair. My first reaction is all *hell yes and thank you, Jesus*.

Then I realize this is not just any woman. It's the hot waitress from The Biscuit in the Basket. The one who remembers every order without writing it down. The one who always seems to know when we need something more, or when it's time to drop the check.

The one with the kissable ivory neck and gray eyes that always make me a little stupid. I've never asked her out, because it's rude to hit on a girl who's just trying to get through her shift at work. But man, I'd like to.

"Hi," she says, frowning at me. "Wow. You're wearing a tie."

"Too much?" I ask, my hand flying to the knot of silk at my throat. "I could lose the tie." And, heck, why stop there? If she asked me to lose my trousers, I'd do it. *Anything for you, honey.*

"No, you look very respectful. Thank you for doing this."

I blink slowly. I can't believe my luck. She's my date? "You work at The Biscuit in the Basket," I say stupidly. "But your name tag says *Gail*."

She smiles. "That's right. The lazy manager put the wrong name on it, and then wouldn't redo it for me. But I'm glad you can recognize me without the uniform."

"Well, sure. You look nice. Your hair is different. Fluffier. Wait. Is fluffy a good thing?" I babble.

She laughs suddenly. "Fluffy is fine. At work they make us wear those visor caps. Like we're all golf caddies."

I smile back at her and get a little lost for another moment. And her laugh is terrific. A little husky. I dig it.

"So, uh, are you ready to go?"

That's when I realize I'm blocking her way out of her own door. "Yup, sorry," I stammer, leaping to the side like a frisky goat.

Oh, man. Nobody would call me Mr. Smooth right now, that's for damn sure. I'm glad my teammates aren't here to witness this. I'd never live it down.

Abbi locks her door. "Where are you from, Weston? Is it too far to go home for Thanksgiving?"

"I'm from the eastern edge of Vermont. But I don't have a car, and we have practice tomorrow anyway. Hey—does your family drink? I brought a bottle of wine." I hold it up, along with a bouquet of flowers, too.

"That's lovely of you," she says. "I have a bottle in my car too. I find that where alcohol and my so-called family are concerned, more is more. Although I'm driving tonight, so I can't drink."

"Your so-called family?"

"Well, it's complicated without being terribly interesting. But we're going to my stepfather's house. I mean, he used to be my stepfather and now he's married to someone else."

"Your step-stepmother," I say, recalling her text message.

"Right." She leads me off the porch and down the walkway. "My car is just around the back. It won't take us long to get there. You'll be eating turkey dumplings in no time."

"Sounds good. My body is, like, fifty percent wings and fries at this point. I'm sure you know that. I'm at your restaurant all the time."

"Table number seventeen," she says cheerfully. "The hockey table. Do you know that we prep a different portion of wings depending on whether you guys win or lose?"

"No, really? Why?"

"Because you eat more and get drunker on the nights you lose than on the nights you win."

"Huh. That's very scientific of you."

She unlocks an elderly Honda Civic and opens the driver's side door. "Last chance to back out."

I wouldn't dream of it. I have to remember how to be Mr. Smooth, though, and flirt properly with Abbi. Who knows? After a great meal, we could make this a night to remember. "I'm at your *service*," I say, hoping it sounds a little sexy and not creepy. "Let's get our turkey on."

Huh. Mr. Smooth seems to be on vacation today.

I give myself a fifty-fifty shot at success. But I've faced worse odds. Game on.

THREE

ARE WE REALLY DOING THIS?

Abbi

"So, set the scene for me," Weston says as I drive toward Shelburne. "How much of an acting job do you need? I can be the new love of your life. Or I could be just one in a string of casual boyfriends. Or even just a friend from far away that you brought home to dinner out of pity. However you want to play this is fine with me. I just need to know ahead of time."

"Right, okay." I have to think fast, because I hadn't actually planned this through. I honestly assumed he wouldn't show up. "Nobody keeps very good tabs on me," I say slowly. "So if I say that we've been dating about a month, it wouldn't raise any eyebrows. And that seems plausible without being a big deal, either."

"A month it is!" he says easily.

This isn't nearly as awkward as it could be, thanks to Weston. He's good company, which I already know since I've listened to a thousand hours of hockey smack talk. He has a fun outlook on life.

"Names, please," he demands. "Who am I meeting?"

"Dr. Dalton Ritter is my stepfather. You can call him Dalton. The new Mrs. Ritter is Lila."

"Lila and Dalton Ritter, MD," he repeats. "I'm premed, so he and I could have plenty to talk about. One more question—can I ask why you felt the need for a date tonight? And are there any topics I'm supposed to avoid? Any conversations I'm supposed to interrupt?"

"Well..." I do have my reasons. But Weston doesn't really need to know what they are. "We should avoid the obvious tricky subjects—like politics. But there's no specific issue between Dalton and me."

"Gotcha," he says. "So I'm just here as a buffer? Is it a big gathering?"

"Nope, which is why I need a buffer. It will just be them and her son."

"Your step-stepbrother?" Weston guesses.

"Yeah, and he's a tool. You'll see."

"No problemo," he says easily. "So you might as well tell me about you too."

"Me? I'm just a student like you. I grew up here in Vermont. And I'm trying to finish my degree in three years plus the summer terms I've done."

"Whoa! Major?" he asks.

"Business, with concentrations in finance and marketing."

"Ooh, finance? That sounds hard. I'm currently suffering through Modern Global Markets."

"Huh, I loved that class," I admit. "Plus, the business degree is practical. I'll be on my own after graduation. That's why I accelerated my degree. But it's been *so* stressful. And all my extra time is spent delivering wings to drunk hockey players, so there isn't much else to tell about me."

"Oh, sure there is," he says. "If we're dating, I would know more about you than the basic facts. What's your favorite song? What's your favorite food? What's your favorite color? Give me something to work with."

"Let's see." I chuckle. "Food? Lately just anything that didn't come out of the fryer at The Biscuit in the Basket. My favorite color is orange. My current favorite song is "Ain't No Man" by the Avett Brothers."

"Ooh, good one!" Weston says. "Put it on. Do you want to take the chorus or the verses?"

"Uh, what?" I reach for my phone and unlock it. Then I hand it to him, because Vermont has a law against holding a device while driving. "Go ahead and play it."

"Okay, but you're singing with me. We'll do the chorus together."

A few seconds later the guitar intro starts up. Weston starts clapping his hands with the syncopated beat. "Ready?" he says. And then he launches in.

And it's rude not to join him, right? So I sing along. And we sing *loud*, the same way I would if I were alone.

Weston doesn't embarrass easily, I guess. He sings every word of every verse, and I belt it out too. Three minutes later we've done the whole thing.

"Whew!" he says, leaning back against the headrest. "That was fun. I always sing loudly before tests too."

"Is today stressful for you?" I ask. "This *was* your idea."

He laughs. "Not at all. I'm fine, but you look ready to barf."

Huh. He's probably right. A trip to Dalton's always stresses me out. Although the words *you look ready to barf* were not part of my fantasy date with Weston.

"Don't worry," I tell him. "I won't barf. They're not really worth it. I just have to show my face on the holiday, make nice, eat some gourmet turkey and then it's over until Christmas."

"Fair enough. Where's the rest of your family? Out of state?"

"Well..." Oh man. I was hoping he wouldn't ask. I swallow carefully before speaking my truth. "This is actually all my family."

"Oh," he says quietly. "I'm sorry. What a stupid question. Way to put my foot in it."

"No, it's okay. I never met my dad. And my mother passed away three years ago." I can say it smoothly now. For a while there I couldn't really talk about losing my mom. I don't remember the last part of my senior year in high school. I spent it curled into a ball, in shock that my mother had taken my dog to the vet one morning, and then died in a car crash an hour later.

It's not supposed to happen to a forty-year-old woman. But it did.

I clear my throat. "So tell me about you. I bet you come from a huge family."

"Uh..." He chuckles nervously. "It's kind of true. I have a million cousins. And an older sister and a younger brother. Thanksgiving can get rowdy."

"That must be fun. No wonder you like the holiday—it must be a huge party. How big is your table?"

"Big," he says. "And my Aunt Mercedes practically has to drive an eighteen-wheeler to shop for Thanksgiving."

"I can't even picture it," I say. Although I've always wanted to be part of a big family. My mom didn't marry Dalton until I was twelve. So for years it was just the two of us, living in various run-down apartments around the greater Burlington area.

My mother had been Dalton's receptionist. He married her about eighteen months after his first wife left him. They were married for six years. So now he's on wife number three.

I moved out about ten minutes after his recent wedding.

Dalton isn't a monster. But I am not his child, and neither

of us ever did a good job of pretending differently. He owed me literally nothing after my mother died. She had no assets to speak of. She cut back her working hours after she married him, because he wanted her to have time to take care of his home, and to cook and to entertain.

My mother *loved* this arrangement. She learned to play tennis. She went out to lunch with friends.

What she didn't do was buy a life insurance policy. Or put any savings in my name. And since my mother entered her marriage with no assets, save for a beat-up car and a nice collection of 90s music on CD, there was nothing for me to inherit.

I get a lot of financial aid from the university because my mother passed away. But Dalton pays a few thousand dollars every year toward my books and fees. He didn't want to pay for me to rent an apartment, though. "Seems silly when you could live in your old room," he'd said.

That was a generous offer, but it didn't feel like a real option for me. So I work a lot of hours at the Biscuit, and I'm going to graduate a year early.

"What was Thanksgiving like?" Weston asks me. "Before? With your mom?"

"Oh!" I say stupidly. But it's been so long since I thought about this. "When I was a little girl, it was just the two of us. We'd get up and watch the Macy's parade from start to finish. And then mom got KFC chicken, mashed potatoes, and corn. She made the pumpkin pie, though. From scratch. My mother was an impractical person. Back then, she didn't cook all that often, but she would bake the most exquisite things. I didn't mind. And I really loved the ritual of Thanksgiving."

"I bet," he says. "The ritual is half the fun. Maybe more than half."

We both go quiet for a few minutes after that. I'm picturing one of our small apartments, with its ugly green carpet and the sagging sofa. The truth is that I would give anything to go back there one more time. My whole childhood, I never had any cause to doubt my mother's love. Even when she married Dalton, I still knew I was her number one.

"Sorry," Weston says quietly. "Didn't mean to bring you down. Do we need another song?"

"Too late!" I pull into Dalton's grand driveway. "We're here already." I park behind Lila's shiny BMW and put the car in park.

"Hey." Weston turns to me in his seat, and makes no move to get out. "It's never too late for a song. I sing loudly and badly whenever the mood strikes."

Wow, is my only lucid thought. Those blue eyes are quite debilitating at close range. Weston Griggs is in my car. For the next couple of hours, he's my Thanksgiving date.

"Once more for luck," he says, hitting the play button again. The Avett Brothers launch into the intro again.

"Are we really doing this?" I laugh.

"We really are."

Then we both open our mouths and launch into the song. This time I'm not driving, so we can watch each other. I'm sure I'd feel self-conscious if Weston weren't hamming it up like a drunk karaoke singer.

He's even dancing a little in his seat. It's so ridiculously cute that I can't help but giggle my way through the song.

Oh God, I'm *giggling*. Just like the girls who are always perched on his knee after hockey games. I get it now. Giggling makes more sense when Weston Griggs is smiling at you.

We're both red faced and laughing as the song ends. Reluctantly, I climb out of my car. Weston grabs the flowers and the wine, and then wraps an arm around my shoulders as we approach the house.

It feels—*wow*—really nice. He's naturally talented when it comes to this fake boyfriend thing. He even gives my shoulder a little squeeze just before the front door opens onto my step-stepmother.

"Abbi! Happy Thanksgiving!" she gushes. "And you must be Abbi's young man. I've heard so much about you."

"Really?" he asks with a chuckle. "What did she say?"

Oh no! When I'd called Lila to tell her I was bringing someone, she'd asked polite questions about my "new man." And since I already admired Weston, it was easy enough to provide some details. *Terrific at hockey. Fun person. Lovely manners.*

Praising him came easily to me. But if she repeats any of it, I'm going to sound like a creepy stalker.

But I'm in luck. She gives him a generic smile instead, probably because she wasn't listening to me anyway. "It's good to meet you. Come right in."

"These are for you," Weston says, offering the flowers. "And I brought a bottle of sauvignon blanc."

"How lovely," she says. "Hang up your coats, and meet me in the kitchen. I'll pour you a drink." She leaves us alone in the entry hall of this house, which I've always thought of as Dalton's. Never mine. Not even when I lived here.

"Oh jeez," I say under my breath, realizing I've left something in the car.

"Problem?"

"The wine I brought is still outside."

Weston glances toward the door. "If you want, I'll step outside right now and grab it for you. But I have a better idea. You could think it over."

"What's that?"

"Leave it out there for now. And you and I can drink it *later*," he says, his voice richening to a suggestive pitch. "If you're into that."

Wait. Now hold on a second. Did Weston just proposition me? For *real*? I might do a happy dance right here on Lila's fussy new rug.

"Hello, sir," Weston says in the next breath. "You must be Dr. Ritter."

And sure enough, my stepfather is right here with us, reaching out a hand to shake Weston's. "Call me Dalton," he says.

They introduce themselves to each other while I stand here feeling befuddled. A second ago—when Weston suggested we save the wine for later—it felt so *real*. My mind offered up a few naughty ideas on command.

But now I realize that Weston probably saw Dalton approaching and whispered to me because it made us look like a convincing couple. Just a hot hockey player having a private moment with his girlfriend, right?

That has to be it. Weston is just doing his best to nail this acting job.

And it's too damn bad. Because white wine and a hookup with Weston Griggs would be the most fun I've had since...ever.

"Abbi?" Dalton's voice breaks through my reverie. "Are you coming?"

"Yes," I say quickly.

Weston takes my hand in his and gives it a friendly squeeze. And that feels nice, too.

It's all pretend, Abbi, I coach myself. *Don't you forget it.*

FOUR

MR. SMOOTH HAS FLED THE BUILDING

Weston

Mr. Smooth must be losing his touch. I nearly propositioned Abbi under her stepfather's nose. Awkward much?

Now Abbi is looking at me like she doesn't quite know what to think. And who could blame her? I should have been more patient before breaking out my *hey baby, let's drink wine and dance the naked tango* speech.

This girl, though. She makes me a little stupid. I've got to pull myself together.

After hanging up our coats, I follow Abbi and her stepfather through a fancy-ass house to a gleaming kitchen. "It smells amazing in here," I say, because it does. "Is there anything I can do to help?"

"Not a thing," Lila crows, the corkscrew in her hands. "Would you like a glass of wine? I also have beer."

"I'll have a glass at the table," I say. "I don't drink much during the hockey season."

"Unless you lose a game," Abbi points out. "Then it's like

29

the whole team is on fire and beer is the only thing that will extinguish it."

I let out a bark of laughter because she's right. "Good thing we don't lose very often."

"Good thing," she says with a little toss of her head. Then she smiles at me, and this weird date feels like the smartest thing I've ever done.

Sometimes you just have to put yourself out there in the universe, you know? Hang up a flyer and see what happens. Maybe the cutest girl at Moo U will call your name.

We make some small talk in the kitchen for a while, until Lila announces that dinner will be served momentarily. Abbi and I help to ferry several dishes through to a dining room with a large round table containing five chairs, five gleaming china plates, and enough silver and crystal to stock a palace.

I pull out Abbi's chair for her, and she gives me a glance of unguarded appreciation.

Yeah, Mr. Smooth is back. And he's going to close the deal later.

I sit down beside her. And that's when an unfamiliar guy sort of slumps into the room. Midtwenties. Dark, shapeless hair. Beefy face and body. He wears the half-alert expression of someone who's just awoken from a nap.

"Who are you?" this creature demands.

I glance at Abbi, and for the first time today, her expression shutters. Interesting.

"My name is Weston Griggs," I say, pushing back my chair and standing again so that I can shake his hand.

He scowls, then leans over the table to shake my hand limply.

"And you are?" I ask, trying to keep my tone polite. At least one of us should be.

"This is Price, my son," Lila says quickly. "And I see you've met Abbi's young man. Price, would you fetch me a glass of ice water and whatever you want to drink?"

He doesn't acknowledge the request. He just narrows his eyes toward our side of the table. "Abbi doesn't have a boyfriend. She never brings anyone home."

Abbi glances down at her plate.

"Price, sweetie, the drinks?" his mother says in a melodic voice. I wonder if she's just saving face, or if she really can't hear how obnoxious he is.

Whatever. I settle back in my chair. That's the glory of visiting with strangers on Thanksgiving. None of the family drama is *your* family drama.

A few minutes later we're all seated, and Dr. Ritter clears his throat. "Weston, do you mind if we join hands for a quick prayer before we dig in?"

"Not at all," I say, offering my hand to his wife on my right. I slip my left hand into Abbi's, and her smooth palm lands easily against mine. I give her hand a quick squeeze. It feels surprisingly natural in mine.

"Heavenly Father, we thank you for this bounty..." He launches into his prayer at a brisk pace, like a man who wants to do the right thing, but also wants to eat his turkey while it's still hot.

I lower my eyes respectfully. But a moment later I feel Abbi stiffen beside me. And then—if I'm not mistaken—there's a bit of violence under the table. As if a feral cat has wandered into the plush family dining room to bite Abbi's ankles.

But I'm pretty sure there's no cat. And when I shift my eyes to the side, Abbi's face has reddened in anger. And she's biting her lip so hard it might bleed.

"Amen," says Dalton.

Not a second goes by before Abbi yanks her hand free of Price's. She sits back in her chair, spine straight, chin held high. But she is *pissed*. I barely know her and I can tell.

Our hands are still joined, so I give hers one more squeeze before letting go.

"Weston, why don't you start the platter of turkey around?" Lila says cheerily.

"Of course." I pick up the serving fork and turn to Abbi. "Can I serve you some?"

"Yes. Thank you." She still looks angry. So I choose a juicy-looking slice of turkey and deliver it to her plate before serving myself. Then I pass it across to her step-stepbrother, who's grinning evilly.

"So where did you two meet?" Dalton asks, passing a plate of dumplings in my direction.

"At work," Abbi says smoothly. "Weston's team comes into the Biscuit several times a week."

"We love the Biscuit. I'm half chicken wing at this point, as Abbi knows. She keeps me from starving."

"That's a nice story," Lila says sweetly.

"Abbi works so hard," Dalton says. "I'm glad that job brought her something good. She works so many hours just to afford that cramped little apartment."

"I like my place," Abbi says quickly. "So convenient for school. Besides, I have to put up with that job for a little longer. In a few months I'll pass the one-year mark. Everyone who makes it a year gets a fat bonus."

"Nice," Lila says. "I guess I'd stick with it, too."

"I will," Abbi agrees. "But you know what's crazy? The weekend bouncers get a bonus at the three-month mark." She rolls her eyes. "There's a lot of turnover in that job. But it doesn't seem fair."

"Pretty easy job, too," I point out. "They just have to stand at the door and look tough."

"They don't even have to stand," Abbi scoffs. "They have a stool to sit on, and free soda or coffee. They check IDs and walk the waitresses to their cars at the end of the night. If I could bench two hundred pounds, I'd switch jobs."

"Sorry, babe," I say, drizzling sauce all over my dumplings. "You aren't scary enough to be a bouncer. Maybe if we gave you a Mohawk and some tats."

Abbi puts a hand in front of her face and laughs. "I swear, it would almost be worth it."

We exchange an amused glance, and I give myself a mental high five for getting her to smile.

"I may never eat again," I declare an hour later as I dry off the crystal goblets that Abbi hands me. "That was magnificent, Mrs. Ritter." It's not a lie. This was my best fake Thanksgiving date yet. "That pumpkin chai pie was exquisite."

She beams. "There's a pie shop in New York City that I admire—Posy's Pie Shop—and I recreated the recipe."

"My compliments to whoever Posy is," I say. "I'm so full I may burst."

"Too full to play some pool?" Dalton asks. "I like to shoot pool while I digest. There's a TV in the game room, too, if you need to keep track of the football score."

I glance at Abbi. "What do you think? Want to play on my team?"

"Sure," she says. "I'm terrible, though."

"Me too," I promise her. "Let's be terrible together."

And we are. Abbi's stepfather knows how to set up complicated shots that quickly leave us in the dust. "It's a good thing

33

I'm on a hockey scholarship and not a pool scholarship," I say as I scratch on the eight ball.

"Good thing," Abbi chirps, and we smile at each other like a couple of conspirators.

I don't mind losing at pool, because I'm winning at life. Every time we step back from the table, there's a new opportunity for me to talk to Abbi. I've woken up Mr. Smooth from his food coma, and put him to work.

I'm putting out all the signals, and she's waving me in. I hope so, anyway.

Life is good, in spite of Abbi's creepy-ass stepbrother smirking at us from a sofa across the room. Every time I miss a shot, he chuckles.

Whatever, punk. Meet me on the ice sometime, and I'll show you how it's done. The guy looks like he's never been to the gym in his life.

As the sky begins to darken outside the windows of the well-appointed game room, I see Abbi sneak a look at her watch. And I remember that there's a bottle of white wine chilling outside in the car, and a quiet holiday night ahead of us, when nobody is expected to work or go to hockey practice.

Maybe Abbi will invite me in when we get back to her place.

After we lose another game, and Abbi checks her watch a second time, I slip an arm around my fake girlfriend. Even this simple gesture is a shock to my system, because she feels so good leaning against me.

And it's not just me, either. I catch Abbi's sideways glance, and it's full of heat.

"Should we head back soon?" I ask, my voice weirdly husky. Mr. Smooth has already deserted me. "Uh, I was hoping to put in an hour or two on that...anatomy paper I told you about."

"Oh, sure." She licks her kissable lips. "No problem."

"What's the paper about?" Dr. Ritter asks. "I used to teach anatomy to the first-year med students at Moo U. Are you premed?"

Well, fuck me. Why did I have to invent an assignment? And why did I pick *anatomy?* I don't have a paper due. My subconscious is obviously hung up on exploring Abbi's anatomy. *Thanks, brain.*

"I am premed. And my topic is, uh, the spinal cord," I say quickly. "And which parts affect which, uh, motor skills."

Abbi's smile widens. She knows I'm talking out of my ass right now. I can only hope that she finds idiots attractive.

"Step into my office," he says. "I have a skeleton that's really great for understanding vertebrae in 3D."

"Wow, thanks," I say as Abbi hides a smile behind her hand. At least we can laugh about this later.

"I'll grab our coats," she says.

"Abbi, honey?" Lila says as we leave the game room. "Could you come with me a moment? There's a stack of your mother's cookbooks I want to ask you about. Maybe there's something here you'd like to keep."

Abbi's face falls. "Sure. No problem."

Lord, I can't even imagine what this must be like for her. A new woman in her mother's former space. Regretfully, I allow myself to be pulled into Dalton's office for a lengthy description of the regions of the spinal cord.

It's a shame I'm not writing a paper on this. It would be a snap now. The man drones on and on while I nod politely.

"Well, thanks," I say at the first moment that it won't seem rude. "I'd better get Abbi home so I can get some work done."

He claps me on the back. "So great of you to be here today. Abbi works too hard and has too few friends. I worry about her."

"It was all my pleasure," I say, feeling like a chump, because I can't really reassure him. Although I'm glad the man cares about his stepdaughter. He seems like a genuinely nice guy, if a little bland and clueless.

Luckily the phone on his desk rings just then, and I can drop my boyfriend act. I excuse myself and go searching for Abbi. She's not in the foyer. So I venture through the living room and toward the dimly lit kitchen, where I think I hear voices.

"Come on. Move." I hear Abbi say. "Weston is probably looking for me."

"Not until you admit it," a male voice says.

I turn around in confusion. I'm alone in the kitchen. Where are they?

"It's none of your damn *business*," Abbi says, the pitch of her voice rising.

"Did you give it up for him right away? Or did you make him work for it. I bet you just spread your legs for him. Is that it? Are you one of those hockey sluts? Do you let the whole team do you?"

"Get *away* from me!"

All my blood curdles. I spin around again and finally notice a door that blends right into the kitchen cabinetry. Like a walk-in pantry, maybe. I cross the kitchen in two steps and yank the door open.

Price's back is to me, but he's got Abbi caged in against a tall built-in bookshelf, his hands on either side of the narrow space.

His reaction time is slow, so he's just turning his head when I grab him by the waistband of his khaki pants and yank him backward.

"Hey! Fuck!" is all he manages to say before I haul him out of the pantry.

"Shut up," I snarl, shoving him roughly against the refrigerator. I am made of adrenaline right now. I can actually feel blood pulsing against my eardrums, and my right hand is already wrapped into a fist.

"Take it easy," he hisses. "I don't want any trouble."

"Too fucking *late*," I sputter. "You don't *ever* put your hands on her."

"I didn't. We were just having a friendly chat."

Somehow I manage not to punch him in the mouth. I don't even know how. My hand is itching to feel the bite of his teeth against my knuckles.

But some kind of protective impulse makes me glance toward Abbi first. She's watching with wide eyes. And she gives her head a little shake, like she can read my mind.

I grab his shirt instead, my hand close to his throat. "No more friendly chats. You don't look at her. You don't talk to her. Or I will punch you so hard that you'll be coughing up your teeth for days. Even if I break my goddamn hand, it'll still be worth it."

His eyes narrow. "Get your hands off me, fucktard. This is my fucking house," he hisses. "She's the little stuck-up bitch who keeps showing up here so that Dalton will keep writing checks. It will not look good for Abbi if I tell 'em you're a violent piece of shit."

That's when I hear the *tap tap tap* of Mrs. Ritter's heels approaching the kitchen. And I take a quick step backward.

Abbi grabs me by the elbow and turns me toward the kitchen door just as her step-stepmother walks through it. "Oh there you are!" she says gaily. "Abbi, did you decide which books you want to keep?" she asks.

"All of them," Abbi says quickly. "She made notes in them."

Lila frowns, as if that answer isn't to her liking. "I could box them up and put them in the basement, I suppose."

"Thank you," Abbi says tightly.

"Thanks for everything," I say, finding my voice. "We've really got to run, though." *Before I maim your shitbag of a son.* I can hear him behind me, where he's opened the fridge. I hear the pull tab of a beer can as he goes about his shitbag day.

"Of course!" she says brightly. "It was so lovely to meet you. Come back anytime!"

I manage to make the right polite noises as we get the hell out of there. And two minutes later I'm standing outside Abbi's car as she bleeps the locks open with a shaking hand.

"Hey. Can I drive?" I ask.

"Uh, sure. If you want."

I take the keys out of her hand, and walk around to the street side of the car. It takes me a minute to move her seat back far enough that I can fit my body into the vehicle. Then I buckle up, start the car and locate the headlights. I pull away from the curb and navigate toward the main road.

Driving calms me down. It isn't until I reach the intersection that I turn and glance at Abbi. She's sitting ramrod straight in the passenger seat, eyes glassy, expression grim. Like a person in shock.

Right there at the intersection, I put the car in park. It's dead quiet anyway. There's nobody behind me. "Are you okay?" I ask softly.

"Yes," she whispers. "I'm fine."

She doesn't look fine. And it's just dawning on me that I failed her. "If I'd known why you needed a date today, I wouldn't have let you out of my sight."

Abbi glances quickly in my direction, and then away again. But not before I see tears in her eyes. "It's embarrassing. I didn't want to explain."

I put the car back into gear and proceed onto the little highway that will take us back into Burlington. "That sucks, Abbi. And I don't mean to pry. But is there any reason we didn't march his stupid ass in front of your stepparents and tell them that he harasses you?"

She lets out a long breath. "I tried. Before he moved in, I told Dalton that he was always making inappropriate comments to me. And Dalton said that Price was just intimidated by me. That I was so much smarter and more successful, that he was just trying to get my attention."

"That's bullshit."

"Yeah, it is. But he's newly married. He doesn't want to hear me say anything bad about Lila or her thug of a kid. I'm not his daughter, Weston. I need him to help me with one more term at school. And I need to finish sorting through my mother's things, before Lila throws all her stuff away. One year from now I'll be free. Then I'll never have to set foot inside that house again."

"Oh. Shit." That's so depressing. But I can't say I'd make a different choice if I were her. "Is Price the reason you moved out?"

"Yeah." She wipes her eyes. "I'm pretty good at avoiding him. Dalton and I go out to lunch sometimes. That's how I stay friendly with him and avoid Price. But Thanksgiving is hard."

"What about Christmas?" I ask, worrying.

She shrugs. "I'll think of something. A weekend away at a friend's house, maybe. Or—worst case scenario—a pretend last-minute ski trip opportunity."

That's just grim. But I'll be across the state, and in no position to help. "I'm sorry," I say again. But it sounds useless.

"It's really okay," she says. "You put the fear of God into him anyway. Seriously. That was your best bit of acting, by the way."

"Because it wasn't," I snort. "I was ready to rip his face off. A guy like that can't get a woman to talk to him unless he backs her into a corner. And apparently that's okay with him."

"He'll probably leave me alone now," she says, just to sound upbeat. "Thank you."

"You're welcome. Anytime."

And to think that I had a tryst planned for the two of us. That's not happening now. You can't put the moves on someone who only needs you around so that she can keep a slimy asshole's mitts off of her.

Abbi doesn't need another guy trying to get her clothes off. She needs a pay raise and a night off and a new family. And none of those things is something I can help her with.

"But how was the play, Mrs. Lincoln?" I joke. "Those dumplings really were excellent. Just saying."

Abbi laughs and then shakes her head.

FIVE
TINY EGGROLLS, PIGS IN BLANKETS

Abbi

After Weston parks my car, he walks me all the way to the front door and waits patiently while I open it. He's the perfect gentleman.

I already knew Weston was a good guy. My mistake was in thinking that I could pretend—even for a few hours—that my life was the fun kind, with a handsome date and no worries.

"Thank you," I say in a low voice. "I appreciate all that you did today." I still have the shakes, too. I should have known that I couldn't be alone long enough to page through a couple of my mom's baking books without that creep harassing me.

I found a handwritten recipe in one of the books. And it's in my pocket right now. That's the silver lining of this shit show. Every memory I have of my mother is precious.

"It was nothing," Weston says gruffly. "My pleasure. You take care of yourself now."

We stare at each other for a beat longer. Earlier tonight I could have sworn that Weston looked at me the way a guy looks at a girl. With possibility. But all I see now is pity.

He reaches out and gives my shoulder a friendly squeeze. "Goodnight, Abbi. Sleep well." Then he gives me a Westonesque happy smile and turns to go.

Wait, I want to call out. *Stay a while*. But I watch him disappear instead. And then I go inside alone.

When I wake up the next morning, the humiliation hasn't completely worn off. I can still smell Price's hot breath as he loomed over me in the pantry. And I can still see the disgust in Weston's eyes as he flung Price against the refrigerator.

That last bit would have been very enjoyable under different circumstances. I'm not a violent girl, but Price had it coming. And then, as I roll over and sit up in bed, I have a brand-new, awful realization. I forgot to give Weston the twenty-five bucks that I'd tucked into my purse.

He spent the day with strangers and fought off Price. And then I stiffed him.

I let out a little shriek of horror. And then I reach for my phone and start texting.

Abbi: *OMG, I just realized I never gave you the 25 bucks! I'm an idiot. Seriously. A waitress should really know better! I'm so embarrassed.*

To my surprise, he starts to tap out an answer immediately.

Weston: *Hey! I wasn't actually going to accept it. I only put that in to keep the nutters away. Seriously. Well, also because it amuses me to charge for my acting skills.*

Abbi: *Your acting skills are on point, though.*

Weston: *Thank you. If this hockey thing doesn't work out, I'm considering Hollywood. There are roles for dumb jocks, right?*

He's so much more than a dumb jock. But I can't say that without revealing how deep my crush on him runs.

Abbi: *I smell an Academy Award for last night's performance. And I am very grateful. How about I treat you to your next platter of Thai spiced wings?*

Weston: *Well, Abbi, I would be happy to accept this as a token of your appreciation for my fake boyfriend performance. An actor has to eat, right?*

Abbi: *Right. See you soon.*

True to my word, the next time Weston comes into the Biscuit, I bring him a double portion of wings and a basket of fries. He gives me a big smile and a high five. But after that, I avoid him. Because every time I see his smile, I feel sheepish about treating him to a front row view of the horror show that is my life. I just want to forget it ever happened.

Between school and work, I'm busy enough to forget almost anything. November lunges into December. Exams loom. Two waiters quit, which means Kippy keeps scheduling me for extra shifts.

But hockey season is in full swing, so at least I have that. Just because I'm avoiding Weston doesn't mean I've stopped following the team. They've had a great start.

Their biggest matchup in December is against Boston University. And I'm on shift that night, checking the score on my phone every few minutes as I wait tables in the bar.

It's a tense game. It's tied 2-2 with only seven minutes left to play. But then Jonah Daniels feeds a wrister to Lex Vonne, and Moo U gets the lead back. When the buzzer rings, we've won 3-2.

For a long moment I feel pure jubilation. But then it occurs to me that The Biscuit in the Basket is about to be flooded with happy hockey players and the fans who love them. And table seventeen is in my section.

"Hey, Carly?" I tag my friend on the elbow as she passes me. "Switch sections with me? You can have the bar. I'll take your dining room tables. Forty bucks for the trade."

"Wait, what? Are you crazy?" she demands. "Who would give up table seventeen on the night they beat BU? You're throwing away extra money *and* extra hotness?"

"I'm just a little tired," I say. It isn't even a lie, because I'm always tired. "You handle the boys. I'm not in the mood to celebrate. I just want to go home and put my feet up."

"I'm worried about you," Carly says. "You need a vacation, and a one-night stand with a hockey player."

"Well *that's* not likely to happen." And I'm really not in the mood to watch if Weston spends the evening with a giggling woman on his arm—and then leaves with her. I haven't seen anyone hanging on him lately. But a win against BU should do the trick, right? "Go serve beer and shots," I say, nudging her toward the bar. "I'll bring out the last few dinners and go home early."

"Fine." Carly pushes two twenty-dollar bills into my hand. "But we're going to have a talk about this later."

The next time we're on shift together, Carly reports that Weston asked for me. "*Where's Abbi tonight?* He knew your real name, too. Did something happen between you and Weston?"

"Absolutely not," I tell her. "We're just friendly, that's all. And that's all we'll ever be."

"*Okayyy,*" she says, her tone full of disbelief. "But he looked really disappointed that you weren't around."

"I highly doubt that."

A week later, though, I'm sitting in an empty booth one night before closing, rolling some silverware, when somebody plops down on the seat across from me. When I look up, it's Weston.

My tummy flutters immediately at the sight of his clear eyes taking me in. "Hey, Abbi," he says.

"Hey, Weston," I echo. "How have you been?"

"Down in the dumps, if you want to know the truth. I got dumped by my fake girlfriend." He grins.

Um...what? "You can't get dumped by a fake girlfriend. That's kind of the point."

He laughs. "Don't I know it. But you *are* avoiding me."

"Am I?" I ask lightly. "Maybe I'm just busy rolling all this silverware into napkins."

Weston studies me for a second. Then he takes a napkin off the pile and positions it on the table in front of him. He takes a knife and a fork out of their respective bins and lines them up in the center. "Like this?"

"Sure," I say, amused. "It's not brain surgery."

"I'm premed," he says. "So someday I'll get to say that unironically."

"Dr. Weston Griggs has a nice ring to it. What specialty?"

"Pediatrics," he says. "You get to talk to kids for a living." He shrugs, like this is obvious. And, yup, Weston just gets hotter by the minute. "Am I doing this right?" He rolls the silverware up tidily inside the napkin. Then he wraps one of the green tapes around it.

"Looks good to me. But, if I may ask, why are you rolling silverware with me instead of drinking with your friends?"

"Oh, I'm done for the night. My party shift is over. But I had a favor I needed to ask you. Remember how I told you I had this big, fun family, and Thanksgiving was always a blast?"

"Yes." I roll another napkin and wait to hear where this is going.

"Well, it used to be true. But my parents got this really ugly divorce a couple of years ago. And now the holidays are murder."

"I'm sorry," I say quickly. "There's nothing like a little tension during the holidays."

"Yeah." He laughs awkwardly. "I know you understand. But here's the thing—if you told your stepfamily you were going out of town for Christmas with me, then you wouldn't have to see them, right? Free pass?"

"Well, sure. I was thinking about telling them that exact thing." After the words leave my mouth, I regret them. Do I sound like I'm pretending he's really my boyfriend?

He sets down another finished silverware roll, and looks me right in the eye. "What if it were true, though? It's me who could use a buffer this time. My sister is having an engagement party on the twenty-third, which means that my mom and dad have to be in the same room together. You could, uh, come with me." He swallows uncomfortably.

"Really? How would that help?"

"They, uh, like to yell at each other. But if I bring home a new girlfriend, my father will be on his best holiday behavior all weekend."

I think about this for a second. "Their own daughter's engagement party isn't reason enough to behave?"

"Well…" He bites his lip.

Before now, I'd imagined Weston Griggs to be the kind of guy who was always comfortable in his skin. But maybe nobody on earth is ever so lucky. I guess he's just human like the rest of us, because he looks plenty uncomfortable right now.

"Look, Christmas is going to be super awkward. My mom is throwing this party with her new man. That's never happened before. So my father knows he has to show up and be civil, even though he can't stand it."

"Ouch."

"Yeah, it's been three years, but sometimes it's like his anger is all that keeps him warm, you know? I'm making him sound like a dick right now, but he really isn't. He is a super nice guy whose wife left him in the worst possible way. And if you spend the weekend with us, he won't complain to my brother and me the whole time. He'll have to smile and make waffles and small talk. It would be a nice break."

"Oh." I think this over for a moment. "Well, I don't really have plans for Christmas."

Weston beams. "And this would put you out of Price's reach, right? You could just skip the whole sorry holiday."

"I could. But, Weston..." I don't quite know how to ask this question without sounding like a self-centered freak. "This isn't just a ploy so you don't have to worry about me, right? I'm a big girl. I can handle myself."

He takes another napkin and smooths it onto the table. "Abbi, I promise you that I'm truly a guy in need of a date. You should know that there are Swedish meatballs in it for you. My sister made me listen to the entire party menu. I can also promise tiny eggrolls, pigs in blankets, and fancy cocktails. Oh, and hopefully waffles on the morning of Christmas Eve."

That does sound promising. "Is the maple syrup real?" I ask sweetly.

"That's my girl!" He cackles. "It's real, I promise. They

throw you out of Vermont if you serve the fake shit on Christmas Eve."

"Well okay, Weston." His smile makes me feel fluttery inside. Spending a weekend with Weston isn't the smartest idea. My crush will only grow stronger. But even so, I hear myself say, "You've got yourself a date."

SIX

CAN YOU DRIVE A STICK?

Weston

On Christmas Eve-Eve, I meet Abbi at noon outside the Vermont Tartan Flannel Factory. She comes bouncing out of the building right at noon, and stops short when she sees me leaning against the driver's side of her car. Her eyes widen.

"Hey, sister. Something the matter?"

She blinks. "Nope. Not at all. Thank you for meeting me here. You look nice."

"Thanks. You too." In fact, I'm glad I put on nice slacks and a V-neck cashmere sweater. Because my fake girlfriend is wearing a dark red velour dress that my sister would describe as artsy. It looks soft and fluid, like red wine in a fabric form. There's just a hint of cleavage at the top. Just enough of a peek that I'd like to put my face right there and kiss the skin above the neckline of that dress.

She looks delectable.

Abbi opens the hatchback and tosses in a duffel bag and her winter coat. I snap out of it and follow her back there to do the same thing. "You mind if I drive?" I ask. "Since I know where we're going?"

"Sure thing." She holds up the keys. "But it's a manual transmission. Can you drive a stick?"

I snort. "That's like asking a man if his dick works."

"Well, does it?"

I grab the keys out of her hand. "I'll show you," I growl.

She snickers. But the truth is I'd like to show her more than my driving capabilities.

Down, boy. I unlock the car and get behind the wheel, scooting the seat back about eight inches so I can get my legs into the car. In fact, I drove this car once before. But Abbi was so rattled, she doesn't remember.

She's not rattled now, though. She slides into the passenger seat, humming to herself. "I'm so happy to have a couple of days away from school and work. I will go anywhere with you this weekend, so long as it does not involve serving fried food to drunk people."

"You won't have to serve any food," I say as her old engine roars to life. "And hopefully there won't be many drunk people." Honestly, drunk people are fine. Unless we're talking about my father.

In this situation, that could be problematic.

I pull out of the parking spot at the flannel factory. It's in an old brick building on the Winooski River. "What do you do at this place, anyway? How many jobs do you have?"

"This was my fun job," she insists. "My internship here is just ending, and I got course credit instead of pay."

"Cool. Which kind of business major are you?" I head for the highway. Abbi's car is a little sluggish. I wonder if she's gotten it serviced lately.

"I'm doing two concentrations—finance and marketing. I want to work on product development, but when I look at job openings for next year, most of them are in marketing."

"Marketing might be fun?" I say hopefully.

"Possibly," she hedges. "This internship was in marketing, and I spent a lot of time trying to take good pictures of flannel with my phone. But I guess everyone starts somewhere."

"True." Stepping on the gas, I accelerate onto southbound 89. But the needle doesn't budge. "Um, Abbi? I don't think your speedometer is working."

"Oh, it's not. You have to just watch the other traffic and blend in."

"Okay." I chuckle as I ease back into the right lane. "Any other quirks I should know about?" She insisted it would be a waste of money to use a rental for the weekend when she had a "perfectly good" car that just sits around most of the time.

Her idea of "perfectly good" and mine are apparently different.

"Well, the gas gauge is also broken. But you don't have to worry about that, because I keep track of my mileage on the trip odometer."

"Ah, okay?" I glance nervously at the gas tank indicator. "So we don't really have three-quarters of a tank?"

"The tank is full, Weston," she says gently. "You're not going to run out of gas. Not today, anyway."

"Good to know." And it's not like I need any extra things to worry about. I'm drumming my fingers on the steering wheel, wondering whether this whole trip was a colossally bad idea.

Abbi reaches over and momentarily places a hand over my twitching one. "Do we need to sing it out? I could cue up a nice loud song."

"Oh, definitely," I admit. "At some point. Why don't you find us something seasonal to listen to?" I like holiday music. Or at least I used to, in the Before Times.

"Good idea," she says, grabbing her phone to scroll through the available tunes. "I'll find something."

I glance briefly toward the passenger seat, where the sun illuminates her silky hair. We're cruising down 89 South toward my corner of Vermont. It's the day before Christmas Eve, and the highway is empty, even for Vermont. There's crisp white snow blanketing the landscape.

There's beautiful scenery everywhere, especially on the passenger side of the car. I'd just like to take a gulp of her.

But I won't, of course. "Hey, Abbi? We'll probably have to share a room. But you can trust me to be a gentleman."

"I know that," she says easily.

"One of the rooms has two sets of bunk beds in it, and that's probably the one we'll get anyway. You can have first dibs." I can count on my brother to claim the other room with the double bed in it.

"Thanks," she says, still scrolling. "Tell me where we're going, anyway. I never drive around Eastern Vermont."

"It's nice there," I promise. It's the one good thing I can say about this weekend—the accommodations are a good time. "My dad's place is right on Lake Morey. It's a cool old lodge that has been in his family for generations. They used it as a summer lake house."

"And he lives there year-round, now?"

"Yeah. He did a big renovation and winterized the place. But we left the bunk room the way it was, because he likes it when we bring friends home." Although I usually do that in the summertime, when Dad's place feels less claustrophobic.

Abbi turns on a playlist. It's a cappella Christmas music by *Straight No Chaser*. But the volume is low, so I guess we're not singing off my tension yet.

"Now, let's take a moment to discuss our story," she says

cheerfully. "Who are the major players, here? What do I need to know in order to play my role effectively?"

"Let me guess—it's a lot more fun to be on the other side of this question."

"Why, yes it is!" She smooths her dress over her knees. "You were right—someone else's family drama is much easier to handle. So what do I need to know?"

I guess I can't put it off any longer. "Well, first I'd like to say that I understand why you didn't fill me in on the whole Price situation ahead of time."

"Because it's weird and embarrassing?"

"Yeah. My situation is pretty bonkers. But there's no way that you're not going to notice. So I'll just come out and tell you that my mother left my father for..." I take a deep breath.

"A woman!" Abbi guesses.

"No way." I snort. "That would have been so much better, seeing as my dad doesn't have any sisters."

Abbi is silent for a second, and I can practically hear the cogs turning in her brain. "Wait," she gasps a moment later. Her voice is hushed, like she's afraid to voice this suspicion aloud. "She left your father for his... "

"*Brother*," I say heavily. "My uncle Jerry is now my stepfather."

Abbi clutches her chest. "Holy crap. That's some serious drama. How did it happen? Wait—never mind. I don't really need to know. But was this recently?"

"Four years ago my uncle got into a serious snowmobiling accident. He was always the wild man of the family. My dad is a nerdy architect, a studious kind of guy, right? And Uncle Jerry is a mixologist, a ski bum, and gave me my first hit off a bong."

"I hope you weren't five years old," Abbi grumbles.

"Nah." I laugh. "I was in high school. But anyway—he gets

into this accident—which was his fault, by the way—and he had all these broken bones and three surgeries. My mom is a physical therapist, and he needed a lot of help. So she took him on as a pro bono patient. His rehab took months."

"Oh." Abbi sits with that for a moment. "And they spent a lot of time together."

"Yup. They didn't just jump into the sack. Apparently they tried to be very civilized about the whole thing. One night my mother just turns to my father in bed and says, *Mickey, I need a divorce. I've fallen out of love with you and in love with someone else.*"

Just saying this out loud makes me want to shudder for my poor dad. "He had a whole life with my Mom, and she just torched it because Jerry was—quote—*more fun and life-affirming.*"

"Ouch," Abbi whispers.

"Ouch," I agree.

"I can't even imagine what that did to your family. Did your dad and his brother get along before that?"

"Not really. My dad was the serious one and Jerry was the screwup. They're five years apart in age, too, so Mom left him for a younger man. Now Jerry and my mom live in the house where I grew up. Jerry basically just moved into my dad's bedroom."

Abbi groans. "No wonder your dad is a wreck."

"Yeah." Not that he's dealing with it very well. He moved out more than two years ago, and he's still boiling with anger. When my sister suggested he go to therapy, he flat-out refused."

"Will they both be at this party tonight? Your, um, uncle and your mom?"

"You bet. Jerry would never miss a party. He probably invited half the upper valley. There will almost certainly be a special cocktail for the occasion, and he'll give a long speech about how the drink is perfect for my sister's personality, or some shit. He likes the spotlight."

"Okay," she says gamely. "We'll smile through it and make a point to drink something else."

That was pretty much my plan too, and I shoot a grateful look toward the passenger seat.

"You're very special, Weston. I never met a guy before who was his own cousin."

I snort. "My family tree is twisted, that's for sure."

"Do you have grandparents?"

"Strangely enough—or not, depending on your viewpoint—my grandpa on my father's side has gone a lot deafer since this whole thing went down. His way of dealing with the chaos is not to hear a lot of it. And never to wear his hearing aid. Can't say I blame him."

"Oh, that poor man," Abbi says. "What a mess. No wonder you don't like the holidays anymore."

She's right—I used to *love* Christmas. But the holidays are just a chore now. On the stereo, the a cappella group is singing "Jingle Bells," and I'm just not feeling it. "It's like I'm numb to Christmas," I mumble. "But Lauren would shoot me if I skipped this party. And so would Stevie—that's my little brother. He's eager to meet you."

"What did you tell him about me?"

"Nothing, I swear. But I never bring girls home for stuff like this. Neither does he. I mean—would you?"

"I tried on Thanksgiving, remember? It didn't go so well."

"Exactly."

"We need a plan," she says. "How close are we supposed to be? Am I just some girl you brought home, or are we dating? How thick should I lay it on?"

I chuckle, because I'd really enjoy watching Abbi turn up

the girlfriend vibes. I wouldn't say no to a fake kiss or two. Although that's not really fair to her. "Look, you don't have to do anything that isn't comfortable for you. They won't believe it, anyway."

"What do you mean?" She gasps in mock outrage. "Am I not girlfriend material? I wore tights and a dress for you."

"No, you goof. You are more lovely and convincing than any other girl I've brought home in three years because—"

"Because you haven't brought *anyone* home in three years."

"Now she gets it. Nothing against that dress, though." I'd still like to touch it—or peel it off her. Although I'm not about to say so.

She clicks her tongue. "Weston, I think you doubt my acting skills."

"It's not that," I promise.

"Still, it's only fair that I get a chance to snow your family as well as you snowed mine."

"Okay." I laugh.

"Let's go with the same story we told my family—we've been dating about a month."

"Fine."

"And what do I win if I can make them believe me?" she asks sweetly.

A kiss. "Um… a dinner that didn't come out of the deep fryer at the Biscuit?"

"Yes! And that bottle of wine we never drank together."

"You're on. This will be fun. I mean—I totally snowed your stepdad. It's only fair to let you compete."

"Exactly."

"But it won't be easy, Abbi. My brother and I have spent the last two years insisting that relationships are for suckers. You can't really live in my dad's house and believe otherwise."

She shrugs. "I like a challenge. Besides, it will make the

party more fun, don't you think? People will be gossiping about us instead of your stepfuncle."

"My—?"

"Stepfather-slash-uncle. Your stepfuncle. Besides—I already have a pet name for you picked out. It would be a shame not to use it."

I snicker nervously. "I'm terrified now. But fine. Two can play at this game. I'm going to call you…" I hesitate. What's a slightly silly but ultimately believable pet name for Abbi?

Honey is too generic.

Kitten?

Sugar pop?

Hmm.

"It's not so easy, right?" She sounds a little smug. "The name has to fit, or people will see through us."

"Eh. I made your stepdad into a believer. And I did it without a pet name."

"Pfft. Price was suspicious of you," she points out.

"Was not," I argue just because it's fun to goof around with Abbi. If she were my only company for the next three days, I'd actually be looking forward to Christmas.

"He was too," she chirps. "Do you want to argue some more? Or are we going to sing something at the top of our lungs? I just found the Avett Brothers singing '*If We Make It Through December.*'"

"That sounds more than appropriate," I admit. "Blast it, baby."

And she does.

SEVEN

A LITTLE OVERHEATED

Abbi

After getting off the highway, Weston begins to wind my little car down narrow country roads, while snow falls gently past my window. It's cozy here in the car with him. I almost wish the trip would never end.

I know Weston doesn't really need me here. But it's obvious he's dreading this party, and that he feels truly grateful for my company. And that's given me a useful, optimistic feeling that Christmas hasn't brought me in years.

Let's face it, if not for Weston, I'd be holed up alone in my apartment right now, thinking sad thoughts about decorating past Christmas trees with my mom. This is so much better than that.

Eventually Weston turns down a driveway between two towering pines. And as we roll toward the house, it's clear he's totally undersold the cool factor of this place. There's a stunning two-story clapboard house in front of us, with a slate roof and a wraparound porch. The doors are painted a cranberry red that's set off against the snowdrifts.

"Wow," I breathe. "It's like parking in front of a Christmas postcard."

"Didn't I mention that my dad is an architect?" Weston asks, hopping out of my car.

"I get it now."

When I climb out, he offers me the keys. "Here. In case you feel the need to make your escape from this looney bin."

"Way to sell it, Griggs." I pocket the keys.

His smile is tight. "Thank you for coming with me, Abbi. I really appreciate it."

"Hey. It's *really* no trouble. I don't mind getting out of town for a couple of days. It's nice to have a change of scenery." That goes for both gorgeous property and Weston's handsome face in front of me. "Look, Christmas is a real drag for me these past couple of years. I get stuck inside my head. It's too much alone time. It makes me sad."

"We have that in common, then," he whispers.

Out of the corner of my eye, I see the window curtain twitch. And maybe that's why I suddenly stand on tiptoes and give Weston a kiss on the jaw.

Whoa. He smells of woodsy aftershave. I have to force myself to rock back onto my heels, instead of leaning in for even more.

He grins. "Is someone looking out the window?"

"Yup!" I give him a big smile. "I'm going to win this thing, Griggs. Now introduce me to your bonkers family. I'm ready."

"Yeah, okay." We share a private smile. "But you've been warned."

As he turns toward the house, he reaches for my hand. As his roughened fingers envelop mine, this feels strangely real. I know it's a game, but his palm feels so solid against mine.

He pushes open the door and leads me inside. There's a shoe rack, so I lean down and unzip my snowy boots. He sets our bags down on the floor and toes off his hiking boots. "Dad? Stevie? We're here."

I follow him into a soaring great room with a huge stone fireplace that takes up one entire end of the room. Some ingenious person has installed a beautiful wood stove insert into it, so the fire inside casts off heat and light, but no smoke.

In front of the fire is a big plush wool rug and a lot of comfortable furniture. There's a coffee table the size of a small country there too, and I'd bet any amount of money that the Griggs men spend most of their family time right there in that spot.

The view is killer. Outside the long row of windows, the lake is visible at the end of what must be a rolling lawn in the summertime. But right now it's covered with snow. Someone has cleared a strip of the ice on the lake, and I see three people whip by on ice skates.

"Whoa. Can you skate right outside your front door?" I ask.

"Yup," Weston says, using tongs to toss another log onto the fire. "Want to try it tomorrow?"

"Maybe," I hedge. "There's no way I could skate as well as you, though."

"That's a good thing, Abbi," he says dryly. "Otherwise the hockey team recruited the wrong person." He gives me a coy smile, and my belly does a little flip.

I don't know how this happened. Suddenly I'm friends with Weston Griggs. And I'm spending Christmas with him in this winter paradise. Not that we'll be making out in front of that roaring fire.

But a girl can dream.

"Hey, Dad!" Weston calls. "You here?"

"Sorry!" comes a shout from the back of the house. And then a big, strong man appears in one of several doorways leading into the room. "I was just finishing up a call. This must be Abbi. Welcome."

My first thought is *wow*. Mr. Griggs is a silver fox. He's a handsome older version of my fake boyfriend. I can see where Weston gets his thick, wavy hair and those intelligent eyes. He steps forward, holding out a hand to shake mine.

"It's nice to meet you, Mr. Griggs," I say.

"Oh, please call me Mickey. The pleasure is all mine," he says with a chuckle. His grip is firm as he gives my hand a polite clasp. "So happy to have you join us for Christmas." Then he steps up to his son and gives Weston a playful cuff on the biceps. "That's for not coming home to see your father ever. But I guess you've been busy."

"It's hockey season, Dad. You know you can come to a game anytime. Where's Stevie?"

"Right here." Another strapping Griggs man steps into the room. Stevie's hair is lighter than Weston's, and he's a little shorter, maybe. But the gene pool has been good to this family. "So you're the mysterious girlfriend." His eyes narrow. "I'm fascinated."

Weston makes a grumpy noise, and his hand finds mine and squeezes. "Be nice, Stevie. Is that any way to greet a guest?"

His brother looks pointedly at our joined hands. "Nice to meet you, Abbi," he says politely enough. "I cleared out of the double room for you two."

"You don't have to do that," Weston says quickly. "You're staying longer."

"Oh I insist," he says with a smirk. "Let me help you carry your bags upstairs."

"We got it," Weston grumbles. "I'll grab our stuff out of Abbi's car."

"Thanks, Westie," I say in a soft, sweet voice.

His brother snorts. Loudly. "Westie?"

"Shut it," Weston says to his brother. "Be nice and offer Abbi some lunch. I'll be right back."

Lunch turns out to be both casual and delicious. We all sit around that giant coffee table in front of the fire eating crusty bread and a meat and cheese board that Stevie has thrown together. There are three French cheeses, two different salamis, several types of little olives, and cornichons.

I'm in charcuterie heaven.

It's also a good vantage point for surveilling the family dynamic.

Weston's dad is a good conversationalist. He tells us all about his newest commission—a teardown in Norwich, where the homeowners scrapped a 1960s raised ranch to build a contemporary mansion. "They're nice enough people, but they have a Frank Lloyd Wright fetish," he says with a smirk. "They keep asking for wood-paneled ceilings everywhere. And I keep trying to talk them out of it, or it will be like living inside a cigar box."

Meanwhile, Stevie keeps sneaking looks at me and Weston. His curiosity isn't very well disguised. So I decide to have a little fun with it. I slide my hand onto Weston's knee, oh so casually.

Weston responds by lifting my hand just as casually into his. We make a great fake couple, if I do say so myself.

But then he casually runs his thumb across the back of my hand, and shivers dance across my skin. For a second, I allow myself to consider what it would be like to be Weston's *real* girlfriend. The minute we were alone, I'd climb onto his lap and kiss him senseless.

He'd probably respond by pushing me down onto this oversized couch, where we'd make out for hours...

"Abbi?" Weston says, squeezing my hand.

"Sorry?" I say, suddenly aware that I've been asked a question.

"Would you like coffee?" Mr. Griggs ask, while Stevie smirks. "I'm thinking of making a pot."

"Yes. Thank you," I say quickly. "Clearly I'm a little dreamy today. Maybe I'll just splash some water on my face." I feel a little overheated too. Maybe it's the fire.

Or maybe it's sexy thoughts about Weston.

"There's a bathroom just down the hall," Mr. Griggs says, picking up the empty charcuterie board. "But why don't you take Abbi upstairs while I make the coffee?" he asks his son. "And find a towel for her."

"Great idea," Weston says.

"I'll just help you carry your stuff upstairs," Stevie says, popping out of his chair.

"No need, punk," Weston says, shutting him down. "What if you minded your own business for once?"

"What would the fun be in that?"

Weston wasn't kidding. Stevie is suspicious.

I can sell this thing. If I'm successful, Weston has to take me out to dinner and split a bottle of wine.

Winning is imperative. I just have to figure out how.

EIGHT

WORLD WAR GRIGGS

Weston

God, my brother is acting like a tool. And my dad seems tense. We just have to get through the party tonight, and then everyone can relax.

"Come with me," I say softly to Abbi. She's the only one in this scenario I can count on to behave. I already feel guilty for subjecting her to the madness of a Griggs family get-together.

She follows me to the staircase, where I step aside to let her go first. And I force myself not to ogle her legs in that dress. "It's the room on the left," I say when she reaches the top. I already put our bags in there.

But when I follow her into the room it looks smaller than ever. She eyes the double bed and then her eyes jump to mine.

"I'll get Stevie to switch with us," I whisper. "I'll tell him…" I pause. "Okay, I have no idea what I'll tell him. I'll think of something."

"No, it's fine," she whispers back. "I'm winning this thing, even if you snore like a freight train."

I bark out a laugh. "I don't."

"How do you know?" she counters, smiling fiercely.

"I guess you'll tell me, then. And I promise to be a gentleman."

"Right," she says crisply. And maybe I'm imagining it, but she actually looks disappointed for a split second. She turns and unzips her weekend bag, pulling out a makeup kit. "Let the games begin."

A couple hours later, after a movie in front of the fire with my fake girlfriend, it's time to leave for the party. So my brother and I flip a coin to decide who's the designated driver tonight.

And I lose. Of course I do.

"You're not even legal to drink," I whine.

"At my own sister's party? Please. Who's going to card me? Not Uncle Jerry. He gave me a beer for my twelfth birthday."

"I can be the driver," Abbi volunteers. "I don't mind."

"No," I say quickly. "You spend enough nights watching other people have fun."

"How's that?" Stevie asks.

"I'm a waitress at the hockey bar," Abbi explains. Then she slips her arm around my waist. "That's where we met. I memorized his order."

"That's so romantic," Stevie says with a smirk and an eye roll. He's not buying what Abbi has to sell. But it's not Abbi's fault. She has no idea how down on love we've all been these past couple of years.

In fact, last Christmas, after my parents had a shouting match on the steps of the church *during* the holiday service, my brother and I literally sat around asking each other questions like: *Would you rather get married or have all of your fingers chewed off by a rabid dingo?*

And we both picked the dingo.

"All right, guys," my father says, entering the mud room. "Let's get this shit show over with."

"Dad," I say, stopping him as he grabs his jacket. "Can I talk to you for a second?"

Abbi slips out the door then, and Stevie does the same.

"What?" my dad bellows. "We'll be late."

I let out a sigh. "What if you didn't go? You clearly don't want to. Lauren isn't throwing a 'shit show' on purpose, you know."

"She's not throwing this thing at all," he grumbles. "It was your mother's dumb idea."

"So you think Lauren should just cancel her party? Or, wait, cancel her whole wedding so that you don't have to feel uncomfortable?"

"Did I *say* that?" he carps. "Don't put words in my mouth."

Now he's glaring at me. All I wanted him to do was check his attitude.

Shit.

"Okay, let's go," I say as lightly as I can. Then I hustle outside because Abbi is in the cold waiting for us. And she deserves better.

The party is held at the Norwich Inn, which is a turn-of-the-prior-century farmhouse-style hotel on the main drag of a classy town across the river from Hanover, New Hampshire. When we arrive, I watch Abbi take in the crackling fire and the two dozen people milling about eating party food and sipping cocktails while Christmas music plays over the sound system.

It's objectively a nice party. And I thaw a little when my sister flounces over with a happy smile and offers her hand to Abbi. "So you're Weston's date for Christmas! I've been dying to meet the woman who would voluntarily put up with him over the holidays."

"I'm getting that a lot," Abbi says cheerfully. "Congratulations on your engagement."

"Thank you!" My sister's eyes dance. "Let's get you both a drink. There's, um, a special one named after me. But we also have beer, wine, and soda. And lots of food."

"Don't worry about us," I tell my sister, folding her into a hug. "Just enjoy your party while it's going smoothly."

"Don't jinx me." She sneaks a nervous look toward my father, who has planted himself at the precise opposite end of the room as his brother. Dad is standing there, hands jammed in his pockets, looking vexed. "I was kind of hoping he'd sit this out if it made him so uncomfortable."

"He's stubborn," I whisper.

"I noticed."

"Don't worry about him," I say, squeezing my sister's arm. "Abbi and I will corner him and tell him bad jokes until he gets bored enough to leave."

"I knew I could count on you." Lauren sneaks another look toward Dad. "I just wish I didn't have to."

Abbi and I get some food, and I bring a plate to Dad. I also bring him a beer.

Then I forget about him for a few minutes and introduce Abbi to my extended family. First there's my mom. "Weston! Hello, lovely boy! And you brought a date to meet your family! This is like a Christmas *miracle*."

Abbi gives me a helpless look before she's swept up into a hug by my mother.

Yikes. I'm going to owe Abbi after this, no matter who wins our bet. My fake girlfriend is gracious about all this weird attention, though. She chats politely with my mom and takes it all in stride.

Then I introduce her to Aunt Mercedes and a bunch of my cousins. They're all like Switzerland, somehow staying neutral in World War Griggs.

The last person I introduce Abbi to is Uncle Jerry. He's set up his mixology table at one end of the room, with a signboard propped onto the table announcing the night's special cocktail: The Lauren.

"What's in The Lauren?" Abbi asks gamely.

"I'm so glad you asked," Jerry says, dropping ice into his pretentious crystal shaker with the titanium lid. "Kentucky bourbon, fresh Meyer lemon juice, simple syrup, and a float of red wine."

"Isn't all bourbon from Kentucky?" Abbi asks. And I have to hold back my snicker.

"Smart girl," Jerry says with a cheesy smile. "Not everybody knows that. This is a special bourbon, too—Knob Creek Reserve. Very round-flavored, with notes of plum and caramel."

Abbi indulges him, watching as he squeezes the lemons and shakes up the juice with syrup and bourbon.

Meanwhile, my dad glowers at us from across the room. He can't stand it that I'm standing this close to my stepfuncle.

Jerry pours the mixture over ice. "And now for the grand finale," he says, lifting a bottle of wine with a flourish. "Watch this." He holds a spoon inverted over Abbi's glass and pours an ounce or two of the red liquid into the golden cocktail. "The wine is suspended there, like a cloud," he says.

"Cool," Abbi says convincingly. "So I shouldn't stir it?"

"No! It's meant to look just like this—with the red floating on top. It's my signature technique."

"Ah, it's beautiful!" Abbi says while I try not to roll my eyes. She takes a careful sip and pronounces it delicious.

I can almost hear my father grinding his teeth from twenty feet away. And when I next glance at him, he's pouring himself a glass of bourbon straight from a bottle. Neat. And not a small amount.

I've got a bad feeling about where this night is headed. And it's only eight o'clock.

For the next hour I try to humor my dad. I really try. And so do my aunt, my sister, and Abbi, who's a champ.

But not only has he been steadily getting drunker, he's practically brandishing that bottle of expensive bourbon he stole from Jerry's bar table, taunting his brother with that sucker.

It's like waving a red flag at a bull. I can practically hear my dad's wheels turning. You do not fuck with a dedicated mixologist's ingredients. Will Uncle Jerry run out of his pretentious unmixed drinks without it? Will he make a scene?

My dad is gunning for it, I think. He gets louder with each passing minute. I've been watching that bottle of bourbon this whole time, too, hoping to snatch it away from him. But Dad holds it in one fist like a cudgel.

"Maybe we should hit the road soon," I suggest. "I've got presents to wrap at home."

"Let me find the ladies' room first," Abbi says.

"Oh, I'll show you where it is," Lauren offers. She detaches from Nigel, her fiancé. "Right back, sweetie."

He gives my sister a soft look as the two women walk away. For a guy named Nigel, he seems pretty decent.

I sneak another look at my watch. We've been here long enough. We've spoken to every cousin and family friend who was brave enough to come over to the chilly side of the room and humor Dad.

So I clear my throat. "Dad, you want anything more to eat? Seems like the party will be winding down soon. We should go."

But my timing kind of sucks, because when I glance at the nearby food table, Uncle Jerry is *right* there.

Dad makes a snarly face. "I'm good," he says. "Lost my appetite. Bourbon?" He holds up the bottle like it's the Statue of Liberty's torch.

"No, I'm the driver. But why don't you let me put that back on the bar?"

"Think I won't," he snorts. "This is top shelf bourbon. Only an asshole would mix it with lemon juice."

I sigh.

"Is that supposed to hurt my feelings?" Uncle Jerry says to the meatball platter.

"Impossible," my father slurs. "Wasn't aware you had any."

"Dad," I warn.

"What? It's true."

Shit. I'm glad my sister has gone to the ladies' room with Abbi, so she doesn't have to hear this.

Jerry turns around, and I brace. "Let him say whatever he wants." My uncle shoves a meatball into his mouth. "He's only making himself sound like a dick. You go ahead and rant, Mickey. Or steal that bottle of bourbon. Whatever floats your boat."

"At least I didn't steal someone's family. Does that make your dick feel bigger, I bet?"

"*Dad*," Lauren gasps from the doorway.

"What?" my dad bellows. "You want to take his side? You always do."

"Mickey," my mother hisses. "Don't wreck your only daughter's party."

"I didn't wreck anything! You two did!" As he shouts, he swings the bourbon bottle wildly.

And it crashes into the brick fireplace and shatters.

"Shit!" he howls. Then, as everyone stares lasers at him, he walks right past me and leaves the room.

My fingers knot into fists, and my first urge is to chase him down and tackle him into the snow. But I get a look at my sister's face, and I don't do it. I count to thirty and breathe.

And then I bend down and start picking up shards of glass off the rug. Because the people who work here do not deserve this.

Nobody does.

NINE

SMELLS LIKE WOODSY GOODNESS

Abbi

I'm standing outside the building when the shouting starts. I'd been about to answer a phone call from my stepfather. He probably wants to wish me a Merry Christmas.

But I silence my phone instead, and listen as the awful sound of glass breaking pierces the silence.

Uh-oh. Poor Lauren. Poor Weston, too. This is exactly what he'd been hoping to avoid. I don't move from my spot on the inn's back porch, because the Griggs family doesn't need one more person gawking at them right now.

But a moment later, Weston's father emerges out of the back door, too.

I'm so stunned that for a beat I just stare at him, open-mouthed. "How could you?" I whisper.

Oops. I shouldn't get involved. I know this. But I'm just so mortified for his family. I turn away because I can't stand to give him any more of the attention he craves.

It's not like I don't understand that he's hurting. It's just

72

that I know how to suffer in silence, like a grown-up. A skill he obviously never learned.

We ignore each other for a couple of very long seconds. I finger my phone in my pocket, and wonder what I could do to help Weston right now.

Meanwhile, the person who should have been helping Weston is pulling a pack of cigarettes out of his pocket and lighting up.

I hate cigarettes. Just like I hate overgrown man-babies.

"Welcome to the family," Mickey grunts. "Things are pretty hairy with the Griggs clan these days."

Oh really? You don't say. But that's all on him. It must be hard work to maintain this level of animosity for—what did Weston say?—three years?

I should just keep my thoughts to myself, I tell myself.

But Weston is hurting because of this man. The whole family is hurting.

Maybe I can't let it go. Some people just need a shake.

"It's hairy because *you* make it that way," I point out before I can think better of it. "This whole situation sucks for you. I get that. But you'd better get a grip on yourself already."

He pulls a cigarette from the pack. "You're young, honey. Talk to me in thirty years."

My blood pressure leaps up. *God,* how I hate men who talk down to women. "First of all, I'm *not* your honey. And there are worse things in life than divorce."

"Sure." He flicks a lighter. "You probably know all about heartbreak and disappointment at the tender age of twenty."

"Hey!" Now my anger is driving this bus. "I only *look* young. Three years ago my only parent was driving my dog to the vet, when they both died in a car crash."

Mr. Griggs jerks backward, like he's been slapped. "Jesus Christ. That's terrible."

"Yeah, I know. But don't feel sorry for me. I don't need your pity. But for the love of God, stop giving your kids so much drama. You're not *dead*." I grab the cigarette out of his hand and throw it into the snow. "Not yet, anyway. So stop throwing yourself a damn funeral."

He drops his head. "Shit."

"Just stop," I repeat, because I'm on a roll, and some people can't take a clue until you shove it in their faces. "Get a goddamn hobby. Get a dog. Join Tinder and find some action. But stop wallowing in self-pity. It's *not* a good look on you."

That's when the slow clap starts. I whirl around and find Weston standing in the snow beyond the circle of light from the porch. His brother is with him, too, and Stevie also starts to clap.

Oh boy. I really didn't mean to lose my temper like that. My face heats like a flame as the Griggs boys finish their ironic applause.

"I'm sorry," I blurt out. "It's none of my business."

"He did welcome you to the family," Stevie says darkly. "That would freak out any girl."

Weston laughs, and the sound is joyous instead of bitter. "It would, right?"

He and his brother look at each other and then laugh so hard that Stevie doubles over.

I edge away from my host—the man I've just insulted. And I step off the porch.

Weston reaches for my hand, and squeezes it. "Well done, Abbi girl. It needed to be said."

Mr. Griggs wouldn't agree, I bet. He stomps past us and heads for the parking lot.

Weston drives us home, his father stewing in the passenger seat.

I'm such an idiot. Weston invited me home with him because he wanted his dad to lighten up for Christmas. But I wrecked it. Now the man will probably avoid me, which means he'll avoid his sons too.

Nice going, Abbi. Great work.

It's deathly quiet in the car until Weston turns on the radio. Naturally there's nothing but Christmas music playing. Weston turns it up, as if he could drown out his father's bad humor with a pop star's rendition of "White Christmas."

"I like you," Stevie says suddenly. He uses a low voice, and I don't think anyone can hear him but me.

"Thanks," I grunt, wondering whether Stevie is going to be creepy. I don't get that vibe from him. Still, it's an odd thing to say.

"I like you for him," he clarifies quietly. "He needs a feisty one. Not all those easy women he takes to bed."

This comment I ignore. I don't want to hear about the women Weston takes to bed. I'm jealous, to be honest.

"If only you were real," he says.

That gets my attention. "What is that supposed to mean?"

"Please," Stevie whispers. "You're not really his girlfriend. I'm not stupid. But it's a shame."

"Careful," I say. "Or you'll get one of my speeches, too."

Stevie snickers. "See? I'm a big fan."

"Dude," Weston says from up front. "Are you seriously giving Abbi a hard time?"

"Nope," Stevie says, shaking his head. "Just telling her how it is."

He's right of course. It's hard to fault him for speaking the truth.

I do anyway.

An hour later, the awkward moment finally arrives—the lights are off. Weston and I are lying side by side in a double bed. Not a queen size. Not a king. Nope. Just me and the hottest man on campus in a double. Lying on our backs. Staring at the ceiling.

I thought this would be awkward because our charade has trapped us here within smooching distance of each other. I never anticipated it would be awkward for an entirely different reason—that I just told his father off in front of God and everyone.

"Look," I say. "I just want to apologize for making tonight more uncomfortable for you. I failed at my job."

"What? No," Weston insists. "You did fine. Better than fine. You told my dad what he needed to hear. We've all tried. But maybe he needed to hear it from an outsider."

"But my job was to lighten him up for Christmas Eve and Christmas."

"Nah, my idea was dumb. I thought I could turn back time. My dad used to love Christmas. He used to make waffles on Christmas Eve morning, with all the toppings. He used to get a Bûche de Noël from the bakery, and hide little presents on the tree. This year there's not even a Christmas tree in this house. It's like he's given up."

"I'm sorry," I say softly.

"Don't be. You weren't wrong about him. You told him how it is."

"I sure did. Loudly."

We both chuckle.

Beneath the covers, Weston uses his toe to nudge my toe. "Just so you know, I got my fake girlfriend a Christmas present. It's kind of a joke, though."

My heart skips a beat. "Just so you know, I got my fake boyfriend a present, too. Also a bit of a joke."

"What did you get me?" he asks immediately.

"You think I'd just *tell* my fake boyfriend his gift before Christmas? Think again."

We laugh, and suddenly this isn't so awkward. Because something unexpected has happened between us—we really became friends. That's how it goes when two people allow each other to see all the dark shadows of their lives. They bond.

And I like it. I need friends. Who doesn't need friends?

"Goodnight, Abbi," he says with a yawn.

I relax against the pillow as the awkwardness between us seeps away for good. It's comfortable here in bed with Weston. He's warm and cozy and he smells like woodsy goodness. "Goodnight, Westie."

There's a soft snort from his side of the bed. And then peace.

TEN

A WHOLE LOT MESSIER

Weston

Somehow, I don't open my eyes for almost twelve hours. When I finally wake up, it's only because I hear the bed creak as Abbi slides out of it.

My eyes fly open, and there's an awful lot of daylight in the room. "Holy God. What time is it?"

"Eleven!" Abbi gasps. "Can you believe it?"

"Wow. I guess we needed that." I roll over onto my belly and squint at her. She's wearing a cute plaid bathrobe over her PJs, and she has pillow creases on her sweet face.

But as I examine her, she grabs for her crazy hair and yelps. "Don't look. I'm a disaster."

I chuckle against the pillow. "Careful, Abbi. Don't let Stevie hear you say that. If you were mine, I'd have seen you a *whole* lot messier."

Her face goes instantly pink, and I realize that statement sounded all hot and bothered. Which is how I feel, suddenly. It's hard not to wonder what she'd look like in my bed after sex. Especially when I'm lying in this bed, my morning wood against the mattress. Oops.

"Mind if I take a shower?" she asks, grabbing her duffel bag off the floor.

"You go ahead," I say quickly. "I put a clean towel on the shower bar for you. The pink one. And you can leave your bag here if you want. There's all kinds of products in there. And I'll trade you for the bathroom when you come back."

"Okay. Cool." She drops the bag. "Thanks. I won't be long."

"Take your time. Make yourself comfortable."

She leaves the room and I sink back into the pillow. I can't believe I slept a whole night in this bed with hot Abbi. I'm lucky my subconscious didn't give me some kind of freaky sex dream, where I'd wake up humping her leg like a randy Golden Retriever.

For that, I think I deserve some coffee.

When Abbi returns in her bathrobe with a towel on her head, I hustle to shower and shave. She actually waits for me to take my turn, instead of going downstairs. I think she's nervous about facing my father alone.

But I know my dad. Nobody will be more embarrassed than he will over that shit he pulled last night. He'll be nothing but polite to her today.

The minute we hit the kitchen, I know I'm right. Dad puts down his newspaper and springs off his stool. "Coffee? Did everyone sleep well?"

"So well," Abbi says politely as I pull out a counter stool for her. "I haven't slept so late in ages. Maybe ever."

"Abbi works two jobs and goes to school full time," I point

out. I know I'm laying it on awfully thick. But I'm proud of her, which is weird, because we haven't known each other very long. My fake girlfriend is fierce. Her life isn't easy, and I admire her in so many ways.

"Well, you're on vacation now," my father says smoothly. He pours two cups of coffee and slides them onto the counter, along with a jug of milk.

And then? He opens up the waffle iron and tips a ladle of batter in. "We've got bacon and sausage in the warming drawer," he says. "And sliced strawberries, maple syrup, and whipped cream."

"Wow," I say slowly. That's what he used to make on Christmas Eve. Back in the Before Times. "Thanks, Dad."

"No problem." He flashes me a quick smile, but it's gone in an instant. "In case you're curious, I already called your sister to apologize. She's still mad, though."

When he turns his back, Abbi and I exchange a surreptitious glance. Of course Lauren is still mad.

"I told her it was probably a good time to ask for a wedding gift. So she did, although it wasn't what I was expecting."

"Okay, I'll bite. What did she ask for?"

His chuckle is dry. "She wants me to go to counseling."

Oh wow. "And?"

"I told her I'd go. To make her, uh, feel better."

"And maybe you as well?" I suggest.

He shrugs. "I guess we'll find out. I'm buying them some of their dishes too. Just as a backup plan."

Abbi giggles into her coffee mug. She drinks it black, I notice, and file that information away for later. A guy should know how his woman takes her coffee.

"Anyway," my dad continues. "I'm headed to the office for a couple hours." He pops a slice of strawberry into his mouth before setting the serving dish onto the counter in front of Abbi and me.

"Wait, you're working on Christmas *Eve*?" I ask.

"Westie," Abbi says gently. She lays a hand on top of mine, and her smooth fingers feel sweet against my skin. A prickle of awareness settles over me. I like her touching me. I like it a lot. "That's what a man says when he isn't quite done with his Christmas shopping."

My dad chuckles. "She's a quick one, Weston. Nothing gets by Abbi. Remember that."

"Oh, I will," I say, playing along. I lift my hand from under hers, and then wrap my arm around her instead, because I'm Mr. Smooth.

She leans against me, also playing along. And doesn't *that* feel nice.

Uh-oh. It feels a little too nice. My dick is confused now. Little Mr. Smooth doesn't know that this is just a charade. He did not get the memo.

Mayday. I've got another day and night to be this close to Abbi. She smells like flowers and coffee and good times. By bedtime, I'll probably have to ice down my dick if this keeps up.

Luckily, the waffle iron beeps, and I let go of Abbi to fetch some plates and silverware.

"That smells amazing," Abbi says as my dad opens the waffle iron. "Mmm!"

If she moans while she eats, I'm a dead man. Quick—I need to find us an activity for the day. Something that won't involve us cuddled up on a couch watching a movie together. I need more separation than that.

I need to cool the fuck down.

ELEVEN

MERRY CHRISTMAS, ABBI

Abbi

"Okay, Abbi. Now we're going to put these boots into the bindings."

We're standing outside in the snow together. It's a crisp, sunny day, and I'm decked out in borrowed cross-country ski gear. Weston had asked me if I wanted to try it. In a moment of foolish bravery, I said yes.

This could go poorly. But what does it matter, right? There's nobody around to see me fall.

Except for the hottest guy at Moo U.

He kneels down in the snow. We're wearing matching LL Bean snow pants from the Griggs family stash. "Put your toe right here." Weston lifts one of my boots in gentle hands and guides it onto a cross-country ski.

But naturally, I begin to wobble. And my choices are to either grab Weston's head or fall over in the snow.

I choose Weston's head. He chuckles as I put him in some kind of new wrestling hold in order to remain vertical. But he carries on, setting my other foot into the other ski, while I cling to him like a doofus.

"You said this was easy," I accuse, finally letting go of his head. I can't help but notice how soft his hair is. I want to sift my fingers through it.

He stands up and smiles at me. "It *is* easy. Just stand there a second while I put my skis on."

"Easy for you to say. I'm regretting all my life choices right now."

Weston had asked me whether I wanted to ice skate—which I can do, but not as well as he can—or try cross country. Foolishly, I picked this. And now there are slidey boards stuck to the bottom of my feet.

"Almost there," he says, stepping effortlessly into his own skis. Then he hands me a set of poles with straps on them. "Put your whole wrist through that loop—upward—and then grab the pole."

"Got it. Thanks. If I fall down and break something, we can use these to drag my body back to the house."

Weston cracks up. "C'mon, Abbi. You got this. We're just going to shuffle forward. The track is just over there." He points with a pole toward the trees. "Follow me." Then he scoots off in that direction.

I try to mimic his stride, with each pole alternating sides with my skis. And it's...doable, I guess. I'm shuffling along behind him with tiny little strides, taking care not to fall down.

When we reach the tree line, I see the track. It's a flattened path in the snow. And off to the side there's a set of two grooves through the snow, side by side. "Is that where we put our skis?"

"Yup," he says. "You don't even have to steer. Let the track do the work. Go on. Try it."

Gingerly, I slide in, one awkward ski at a time. When

Weston leads me forward again, though, it's definitely easier. I scoot each ski forward in a rhythm, poling with my hands to propel me along.

"Yesssss!" he shouts. "That's it!"

I move forward on the perfect white snow, pine trees on either side of me. There's a brilliant blue sky overhead. "Okay, this is almost fun."

"Almost?" he snickers.

"Well, I'm slow," I admit. "I could probably walk faster than I'm skiing right now."

"With all of five minutes' experience, I really would have expected better from you."

"I know, right?"

He leaves the track and glides up next to me on the path. "Do me a favor and try to ski like a gorilla."

Still striding, I throw him a quick glance. "Why? So you can blackmail me with the pictures later?"

"Thanks for that brilliant idea, but all I was trying to do was lengthen your stride."

"Show me," I demand, stopping midstride.

"Sure thing. Look. I'm bending my knees a little bit, reaching my arms out, my upper body tilted forward. And…" He starts to move. "Hoo hoo hoo hee hee," he says, pursing his lips like a gorilla.

I can't help it. I giggle just like his female fan club at the Biscuit after a game.

"Hoo hoo hoo," he says, striding forward. And—fine—I can see how the posture assists his skiing. He circles back, the gorilla noises growing louder. He doesn't even stop when a man skis by him with a tiny kid in a pack on his back.

Yup. I'm a little more in love with him than I was already. Any hot guy who will voluntarily humiliate himself to teach you to ski has got to be a keeper.

"Your turn." He stands up straight and smiles at me.

"All right," I agree. "But only because you're a really good sport."

"Nah," he says. "That title goes to you this weekend. Now let's see it. Show me some gorilla, Abbi."

I skip the noises. But I lean forward and start skiing again.

"Yeah! There you go." He glides forward and ignores the track in favor of skiing next to me. We press on as the path turns around the lake. I can see skaters out in the center, and steam rising from the little metal chimneys on several of the ice fishing huts.

"You do any fishing?"

"Nope," he says. "Too boring. Ice fishing is for old guys with beer guts. They just sit in there and drink all day."

We ski side by side, and I start to get the hang of it. But it's work. I'm puffing along now, and a light breeze sends snow glittering from the pine boughs down onto the path. "How long is this trail, anyway?"

"Oh, not long. About ten miles."

"Omigod," I squeak, and he laughs.

"It's two miles, tops, Abbster. I'm just teasing you. And we can turn around anytime you want."

"Good to know."

"Of course, then we'll go skating," he says.

"Uh-oh."

"You'll love it. I'll bring hot chocolate."

"Oooh. Okay!"

He laughs.

It's a really good day.

No, it's a *great* day. We ski, we skate, and we hang out in the sunshine drinking cocoa. I feel like I'm on a vacation from my real life. There are no shifts at the bar, and there's no homework.

There's no grabby step-stepbrother.

That night's dinner is another charcuterie fest in front of the fire, this one featuring—alongside the cheese—slices of ham and vegetables and dip.

"This is really decadent," I gush, swirling a little glass of red wine that Weston has poured for me. I help myself to another French olive. I feel fat and happy staring into the fire.

"Save room for dessert," Weston's dad says. "I got a Bûche de Noël. But here's a question—do you want to do presents tonight, or tomorrow morning? I'm happy to adhere to tradition, but you all seem to enjoy sleeping in."

"We're all here now, right?" Stevie says. "Let's do it."

"Sure, Dad," Weston agrees, patting his stomach. "I need a spacer before dessert, anyway." He pushes up, off the couch. "Let me get my stash of gifts."

I get up too, retrieving a shopping bag that I'd hidden in the mud room.

Weston returns a couple of minutes later with three gifts: one for his dad, one for his brother, and a big squishy one with a gift tag in the shape of a polar bear. It says *Abbi* on it in red marker, with a smiley face.

And I know my reaction is dumb, because presents don't really matter. I'd give up presents forever if I could spend one more day with my mom. But just seeing my name in Weston's cheerful scrawl does something to me anyway. It gives me an unexpected zap of optimism. It reminds me that life can still deliver surprises when you least expect them.

Weston sits beside me and drapes an arm around my shoulders. "Merry Christmas, Abbster," he murmurs. "Such as it is."

It *is* merry, though. I could be sitting alone in my apartment right now, shivering under the comforter because my landlady won't turn up the heat. But I'm here in front of this crackling fire with a cute guy who likes polar bear gift tags.

Life really could be worse.

Mr. Griggs has given each of his sons a pair of very pricey headphones for Christmas, and they are well-received. And both Weston and Stevie produce thoughtful presents for their dad, too, of the manly variety. Weston gives Mickey a leather fireproof glove for tending that wood stove we're sitting in front of. "So you can stop singeing off your arm hair," my fake boyfriend explains.

And Steve gives him a set of drafting pens from Japan. "It's what all the new kids are using," he says. "You might like them, old man."

Mickey smiles indulgently and gives his son a one-armed man hug.

Then the big moment arrives. I place my carefully wrapped gift in Weston's lap. "This is for you, Westie. I hope you like them."

"I'm sure I will, baby. You know me so well."

Across from us, Stevie actually rolls his eyes.

Damn Stevie. I've only got a few hours left of this holiday visit to convince him.

Meanwhile, Weston tears the paper off his gift like, well, an overgrown kid on Christmas Eve. And when he lifts the lid, he chuckles. "Cute, honey." He lifts a pair of super soft black flannel sleep pants from the box. They're printed with an adorable white dog in profile, who's wearing a cheery red collar.

"Those are supposed to be West Highland Terriers," I explain. "But most people call them—"

"Westies," he says with a laugh. "Aren't you clever?"

Smiling, he drops the flannel in his lap. And then our eyes meet, and we both seem to hesitate at the same time, because couples don't just shake hands when they're exchanging gifts. There's often a thank-you kiss.

And now there's a frozen look in Weston's eyes. Then he seems to shake off his hesitation. He moves, opening his arms.

Now, in my defense, I'm trying to be a better fake girlfriend today than I managed to be yesterday. So I open my arms, too, rotating toward him...

But I'm a beat late, and Weston is already in motion. The result is much more like a collision than a hug and kiss. My lips hit his throat as his face sideswipes my forehead. And I elbow his chest and he sort of crunches me against his collarbone.

At least my yelp of pain is buried in his clavicle. That's the only saving grace to The World's Most Awkward Hug Ever.

"Sorry," we both murmur in unison, pulling back, matching sheepish expressions on both our faces.

I hear a painful snort and turn to see Stevie, who's *dying* of laughter. His face is red and his body is shaking.

Weston, also red faced, puts my gift in my lap. "Open this. I've been dying to know what you'll think." He winks at me, like we're sharing a joke. "It could really go either way."

"Okay!" I say, grateful for the distraction. I remove the polar bear and set it beside me. I don't even know why I like it so much. Then I rip the paper off what turns out to be a hunter green Moo U hockey zip-up sweatshirt with a *wonderful* piled fleece interior. "Ooh! Cozy," I say. I've seen these before but they're spendy, so I don't own one.

"Don't miss the back," Weston says with a sly grin.

I flip over the shirt. And there it says GRIGGS in block letters right over his jersey number.

I laugh. Loudly. "So I'm supposed to parade around campus with your name on the back of my shirt?"

"Wouldn't that be an honor?" Stevie asks, his voice a challenge. "I mean—rumor has it that you've taken the most eligible bachelor in Burlington off the market. Unless I'm wrong about that?"

"Oh, you're right," I say quickly. "But this isn't 1965. These days a girl likes to stake her claim with a tattoo. I mean, it doesn't really say *love* unless you bleed for it, am I right?"

Weston and his dad both crack up. Mr. Griggs gets up, pulls on his new fireproof glove, and feeds a log to the fire.

And that reminds me. "I have something for you, Mickey."

"You do?" He straightens up, a look of surprise on his face.

"Absolutely. It's right here." I pull out my other wrapped gift. "My mother was big on hostess gifts. She never stopped by anyone's house without a complete set of dishtowels, or a handmade candle." I'm babbling now, because I can't seem to shut up when I'm talking to Mr. Griggs. "So I wanted to bring you a thank-you gift, and the company where I did my internship makes nice stuff." I hand over a wrapped present. "It's just a little thing."

Mickey gives me a funny smile and rips off the paper to find a pair of wool flannel slippers inside. "Thank you, Abbi. These are great."

He's not wrong. They're charcoal gray with blue stitching, because Vermont Tartan makes snazzy things, especially for the forty and older set. "I'm glad you like them. It's a nice local company, and I hope they're around forever."

"Well…" He sets the slippers down on the floor and slips his feet right into them. "As it happens, I have a little gift for you, too."

"Oh, you didn't have to do that." I feel my face heat, because I never meant to put him in this position. And now

I'm bracing myself for whatever emergency thing he's just thought of to hand me.

"I know," he says. "But this is for you, because I bet you could use it." From beside his chair he pulls a shiny gift bag, with tissue paper sticking up from the top. He stands and hands it to me.

To my surprise, there's a gift card tied to the handle reading *Abbi*.

"Oh," I say stupidly. "Wow."

"Go on," he says quietly. "Open it."

Nervously, I pluck the tissue paper off the top. And when I reach inside, my hand collides with buttery leather. I pull out a gorgeous new satchel, large enough for a laptop computer. It's cut in a curvy, feminine style, in cognac leather.

I don't know if I've ever held such a gorgeous bag. And when I flip open the top, there's even a padded laptop pocket inside. "This is...wow." I babble. "So *fancy*. It even has that new bag smell."

He gives a startled chuckle.

"Way to upstage me, Dad," Weston jokes.

"Well, Abbi," his father says. "I gave one of these to my daughter the year she graduated from college. She needed an upgrade from her book bag, to look more professional. And I thought you could use one, too. Especially..." He clears his throat. "If you don't have a parent handy who can give you one."

"Oh," I say, looking up suddenly. And he's watching me with a father's compassion in his eyes. "Thank you," I say, but I choke on the words. It's such a generous thing to do, and for such a lovely reason. And—oh shit. Tears have sprung into my eyes.

I look back down at this gorgeous piece of craftsmanship and try to hold it together. But my next breath comes out as a sob. Because it's Christmas. And I'm graduating this spring. And my mom won't be there to congratulate me at all.

"Oh nooo!" Weston croons. He drops an arm around my shoulders, and this time he manages to pull me into a hug without violence. "You broke my girlfriend on *Christmas*. Quick! Someone put on a funny movie."

I laugh and cry at the same time, and Weston pats my back.

"Th-thank you," I stammer at Mr. Griggs when I'm able. "It's just gorgeous."

"You're welcome," he says, looking a little uncomfortable at the mess he's created of me. He gets up to find a box of tissues, which I need, badly.

And then Stevie puts on *Home Alone 2*, and we all watch it.

Somehow, I end the evening smiling.

TWELVE

DID SHE JUST MOAN MY NAME?

Weston

I look around the living room as the movie winds down. We've all had cake, and we're half-dozing in front of the TV.

It's hard to believe, but Dad saved Christmas just before the buzzer. It's not that I really needed the Christmas Eve waffles or the cake shaped like a log. I'm a big boy. But it's nice to see him trying to find joy again.

Abbi gets the assist, too. She kicked Dad's ass last night and it made all the difference. He's a new man today. A very contrite one.

My fake girlfriend is quiet now, tucked up beside me on the couch, near enough that I can smell her shampoo. She's smiling, too. Whenever Macaulay Culkin pulls off another feat, she laughs.

I already knew Abbi was resilient. I knew she was alone in the world. But I didn't really understand how that must feel until I watched her lose it over a gift from my dad.

It's humbling to think about how easy I've really had it.

Sure, my parents had an ugly divorce. But even that drama will be old news eventually.

My gaze wanders over to my father, who's yawning as the credits roll. "I'm going to bed, boys. And Abbi. Happy Christmas."

"Happy Christmas, Dad. Thanks for everything tonight."

My brother and Abbi chime in with the same, and Dad just shrugs. "My pleasure. Sleep well. Sleep late. We'll have brunch before you guys shove off to Burlington," he says to me.

After he goes, my brother puts on another movie. And then he nods off.

I poke Abbi's knee gently to get her attention. And then I point at Steve, who looks particularly stupid with his mouth hanging open.

Abbi squints at him. And then she leans in so close to me that I feel her silky hair tickle my ear. "He's faking," she barely whispers.

What? I glance toward Stevie again, but I can't really tell.

"Why?" I mouth.

"To spy on us," she whispers.

I chuckle, because that is definitely something Stevie would do. Well, I'm not going to give him the satisfaction. "Stevie," I bark.

His eyes open with exaggerated stubbornness. "Whoops, I guess I nodded off."

Yeah, he was totally faking it. "We're going up to bed," I say with a sleazy wink. "Don't hurry to follow us."

Stevie reaches for the remote control and clicks off the TV. "Actually, I should head to bed too. It's important to get enough sleep."

Abbi gives me a pointed look that asks, *Can you believe this bullshit?*

We all get up. Abbi carries our glasses to the kitchen, and

Stevie checks the fireplace to be sure it's sealed up tightly. I turn out the lights. Then we all walk upstairs in a line. "Sleep tight," Stevie says outside of the bunk room. Then he gives me a grin and goes inside.

Okay, so now this is back to being awkward as fuck. Abbi and I find ourselves in close quarters a moment later, whispering to each other. And we both know Steve is right on the other side of the wall.

"He's so smug!" she whispers. "I don't like to lose a bet."

"Easy, killer." I put my hands on her shoulders and chuckle. "It was never a fair fight. This doesn't reflect badly on your girlfriend skills. It's all on me."

"Pfft," she says. "*It's not you, it's me.* Girls love hearing that."

I crack up, because Abbi is hilarious. And while I'm distracted, she darts away to claim the bathroom before either Stevie or I can get to it.

When I go out into the hall, he's standing outside the bathroom door, arms crossed, waiting. "Your so-called girlfriend is hogging the bathroom."

"My *girlfriend*," I say with exaggeration, and no small amount of loyalty, "can take her time."

Stevie just smiles. "She's the best, Weston. I can see why you're actually tempted."

I open my mouth and then close it again. Because I *am* tempted. But I can't discuss this with my brother, because I have a ruse to maintain.

So I leave him there and head downstairs to use my dad's bathroom instead.

Fifteen minutes later, I'm wearing my brand new Westie pajama pants, and lying carefully on my side of the bed, as Abbi slides in beside me. The bed wiggles a little as she arranges herself at as polite a distance as she can manage in this small space.

I'm wide awake, and overly conscious of how close we are together. What would Abbi do if I rolled over and kissed her?

She'd kiss me back, that's what. I know this on a gut level. But I'm still not going to do it. I invited her here as friends. And I promised her that I would be a gentleman. And it's not fair to change the rules just because I'm attracted to her.

The silence seems really loud. I can tell Abbi is lying there, much like I am, too aware of the confined space to be restful.

"Thank you for the kickass pants," I say. "They're pretty awesome." *And so are you,* I want to add.

"Thank you for the fuzzy, yet slightly egotistical sweatshirt," she whispers.

I chuckle into the darkness. "They all have player numbers on the back, you realize. I didn't invent that."

"Of course you chose your own number, though," she says in a teasing whisper.

"Well, sure," I argue. "If you're going to have some guy's name on your back, why not mine?"

"I'm surprised it wasn't sold out already," she says with a giggle.

"They went fast," I insist. "That's what I'm telling myself anyway."

"Uh-huh. I'm going to wear it tomorrow in front of Stevie. This isn't over. I don't accept defeat easily."

"Yeah, I'm getting that." I'm realizing that it only took a couple of minutes for the awkwardness to blow over. Abbi *is* the best. She makes everything fun.

"He's right on the other side of this wall, right?" she whispers.

"Yup."

"I have an idea. Did you see *When Harry Met Sally?*"

"Yeah, why?"

"The diner scene."

I'm just processing this as Abbi wiggles a little. The bed responds with a creak. Then she *moans*. "Ohhh. Oh, *Weston*."

Holy... All my nerves stand at attention. Did she just *moan my name*?

She shifts again, and the bed begins to creak in a slow, rhythmic way. She must have braced a toe on the floor. "Mmm-mm..." She sighs. Loudly.

And, wow, it's very convincing. I'm convinced. My dick is also convinced. Suddenly he's up and at 'em, wondering when the party starts.

"Oh *Weston*," Abbi croons. Then she elbows me.

"*What?*" I hiss as the bed continues its erotic rhythm.

"A little help, here," she hisses back.

Oh I'd LOVE to help! my dick screams.

What is happening? My brain and my body are on opposite tracks. On the one hand, I'm mildly amused that Abbi is trying to fake out Stevie with sex noises. It'll never work.

But on the other hand, my body is on board this train. As the bed rocks gently I have no trouble at all imaging myself as the conductor.

I swallow roughly. "You realize you have to keep this up for a really long time, right? This is only a believable scenario if I last half the night."

"Oh, *yes* baby." Abbi moans, before suddenly clamping a hand over her mouth to stifle a laugh. She's amused. She finds this whole thing funny.

I'm just turned on. This is torture.

And then she moves a little closer to me, and my senses all go haywire. But it turns out she's just trying to say something privately. "Jeez, Weston. Even you must be capable of a Christmas quickie. Just play along." Then she increases the tempo of the bed's movements. "Yessss...." she cries out. "Faster."

Then she elbows me again.

Shit.

It's risky to play this game. If I say anything, she'll be able to hear how tuned on I really am. I clear my throat. And then I clench my teeth and think about hockey drills. "Okay, yes!" I say woodenly.

"Is that the best you can do?" She hisses. "Really? You sound like you're watching a game on TV. I suddenly feel sorry for all those women at the Biscuit."

Wait, what? Is she questioning my *skills?* "Oh *hell,*" I grunt. "You did not just say that."

"Yes, *yes,*" she moans in answer. "Let me hear it, baby."

And now it's me who's stifling a laugh. Abbi is fearless, as well as hot. She pushes all my buttons.

"*Weston,*" she moans, and then covers her mouth. I can feel her shaking with laughter.

Time to step up, I guess. "What, baby?" I pant. "You need more? I got more."

"*Harder,*" she manages to yell, but she's clearly laughing over there.

I roll over and brace a foot on the floor. "Oh *yeah,*" I call, nudging the rocking bed into a gallop. "Like that?"

"Yes! Yes!" she moans. "Just. Like. *That...*"

Oh God. My dick is trapped against the mattress. There's some friction from the motion of the bed, and Abbi's breathy moans in my ear. I'm dying, here. "Hurry, baby," I groan.

And I'm not kidding. This torture has to stop. I move the bed even more, until the headboard smacks the wall on every stroke.

"*Westonnnn!*" she shouts.

And it's so, so easy to picture the real thing—Abbi flushed

and climaxing beneath me as I strain against her soft, supple body... "Uhnnngh," I moan, because I'm so worked up. And then I flop down onto the mattress one last time and go absolutely still, which is a necessity. If I move any more I'm going to blow just from listening to Abbi fake it.

I force air into my lungs as the room goes still.

There's no more sound from the other side of the bed, either. I'm expecting a joke, or maybe a compliment on my expert acting skills.

But all I can hear is Abbi's rapid breathing.

And then I push my face into the pillow and smile. Because I think Abbi got a little more than she'd bargained for, too. I hope it keeps her awake. It's only fair.

It's going to be hours before this crowbar in my new pajama pants goes away. She might as well suffer, too.

Happy Christmas indeed.

THIRTEEN

FOUR TIMES MORE AWKWARD

Abbi

"And then what happened?" Carly demands.

"Then his brother believed us," I say, rolling another fork and knife into a napkin. "At least I think he did. How could he not?"

"No—forget the brother." Carly tosses a silverware roll into the bin and blinks at me. "Please tell me this story has a *very* happy ending. Tell me you both turned to one another and started ripping each other's clothes off."

"Nope. We went to sleep." Eventually. The truth is that I faked sleep for a good long time. After hearing Weston moan from close range, I was too stirred up to sleep.

"Abbi!" she shrieks. "Why the hell didn't you have *actual* sex?"

I shrug. "He didn't touch me. He was a perfect gentleman. I don't think he likes me that way."

She blinks. "I do not *believe* this. First of all, does it *really* matter? Anyone who simulates sex for five minutes loudly,

99

with great enthusiasm, is going to be into it. He's a horny college guy."

"But—"

"If you'd just leaned over and kissed him, you could have spent the next twelve hours in pound town. You whiffed it! Someone lobbed you a nice easy pitch, and you let it fly right by. I'm *so* disappointed!"

"Carly, stop it."

She giggles.

But to me, this is no laughing matter. "The thing is, if I leaned over and kissed him, and he really *really* wasn't into it, then I would have made a super awkward evening four times more awkward than it already was."

"Details." She rolls her eyes. "I'm just sad for you and your vagina."

"I'll admit that part of my body isn't really speaking to me right now."

She cracks up.

"But I still don't really have any regrets. Because we're *friends*. Good friends. And that's important."

"I guess." She lets out a dramatic sigh. "But, lordy. One of us should ride that bull before we graduate. We're due for some good times, don't you think?"

"Not sure it works that way," I mumble. Good times are nice, but they don't pay the rent. I have to keep my head down and focus on what's important. Like graduating and finding a real job.

Weston got me through another holiday season without my mom, and I'll always be grateful. But Weston is not boyfriend material. And there's no other guy around here that's half as interesting to me. So I don't see the point of being sad about it.

Although—and I'm not about to confess this to Carly—I've worn my snuggly team sweatshirt, with his jersey number on the back, two mornings in a row. If anyone asked me why I like it so much, I'd point out that the sweatshirt is warm, and my apartment is cold.

But my crush on Weston is stronger than ever now. Becoming friends only made him more attractive to me. He's a good man. I'm lucky to know him. Even if I'd prefer to know him naked.

"Ladies, I have a job for you." Carly and I both look up to find Kippy—the lazy manager—standing over us with a stack of fliers.

"We're doing our job right now," Carly points out. She says this in a cheerful voice, but I can hear the underlying snark that's often there when Carly speaks to Kippy. He's such a tool.

"Yeah, but I need you two to pin these up all over campus," he says. "New Year's Eve is only a few days away. I'll need you both to work late that night, obviously. And these need to be up all over campus by tomorrow morning. You can do it together after your shift."

"After our shift," she repeats. "At eleven?"

"Sure," he says, dropping the flyers onto the table. "Thanks."

Our eyes meet after he walks away. "That lazy motherf—" She bites back the rest. "He knows we're not going to complain."

"It's too close," I point out. Both Carly and I are coming up on our anniversary bonus. "That's why he asked us."

She nods, her eyes flashing. "He could probably ask me for a damn blow job at this point, and I'd do it."

"Carly!" I squeak. "Ew."

She giggles. "You should see your expression. Hilarious."

"I'm repulsed."

"I know! I wouldn't *really* do it," she says, grinning. "But getting this bonus is like a crusade for me, now. It's more than just fifteen hundred bucks. It's an investment of a year. I've earned it. I want it. And no weasel-faced manager is going to get in my way."

"Have you started counting down the days?"

"I'm going to. Tonight. Right after we hang flyers all over the campus. In the December cold. At midnight." She rolls her eyes. "At least the event looks fun." She grabs a flyer and holds it up so I can see.

The Biscuit's Raucous New Year's Eve: Featuring Live Music from The Hardwick Boys
Midnight countdown. Two-for-one wings 6p-9p. Join the party!

"Well, the tips will be great," I point out. "If people are drinking their faces off from nine until midnight."

"Yeah," she says with a sigh. "Wouldn't it be nice to go out on New Year's like a normal person, though?"

I shrug, because I don't even know who I'd go out with.

"Maybe Weston will come," Carly says, her eyes brightening.

"Maybe. The hockey team is on campus already. They don't get a long Christmas break."

"That's right," she hoots. "Your new boyfriend probably told you their schedule."

I roll my eyes. "Don't make me regret telling you that story."

"So table seventeen might be hopping on New Year's." Her smile is brilliant. "Has he called you since you guys got back?"

"No, but why would he?" I shrug.

Her smile goes dreamy. "Because he probably misses you. I bet he woke up the day after Christmas and thought about you. He probably wants to reenact your fake sex scene for real. I bet he's still thinking about it."

"That's not how my life works," I mutter.

"It should be," Carly says, tossing the last silverware roll into the bin.

"How fast do you think we can hang up twenty fliers after work?" I ask.

"Let's hang up ten and recycle the rest," she whispers.

"But if New Year's is a flop, we won't get good tips," I point out.

"Fine," she says, standing up to tie on her apron. "But it won't be a flop. I just know it."

Four nights later, I find out she's right.

There's a sweet spot to waitressing. When the place is dead, I get bored and make too little in tips. But when the place is slammed, the customers get crabby and I get stressed out. In the middle zone is where this job is really pretty great. When the stars align, you can have happy customers and fat tips as the hours fly by.

And then there's New Year's Eve. I've never seen the Biscuit so crowded. Every table is taken, and it's standing room only at the bar. Every available staff member is on shift, and I heard they started a new bouncer tonight just to double up on security.

The clientele is in a good mood, though, and The Hardwick Boys sound terrific. It's tricky to hear the patrons shout their orders over the music, but I don't even mind. The lively atmosphere and the holiday tips make it all worthwhile.

And—even better—table seventeen is chock-full of hockey

players, including my favorite one. Every time I drop off a beer or even pass by, Weston gives me a warm smile.

I'm trying not to pay too much attention. I'm a busy girl. But I haven't been able to stop thinking about him all week. Spending time together as friends has only made him more appealing.

And sometimes? I think he's attracted to me, too. Am I crazy, or does he keep glancing at me? Or did I dream that?

I did. I dreamt it. Weston isn't shy. If he wanted me, he'd just say so.

"He keeps looking this way!" Carly shouts as we stand in front of the bar, waiting for various drinks to be made. "That boy wants you!"

"What boy?" I shout back.

Carly rolls her eyes. "You don't fool me. I'm not stupid. But I think you might be. Don't look, but he's watching you even as we speak."

I don't look, because I don't want to encourage her. I'm deep in the friend zone with Weston, and that's just the way it is. "He's just waiting for his beer!"

"Yeah? Well he looks especially *thirsty* tonight," Carly yells back. "Get on that." She winks as the bartender plunks her drinks down onto the bar. With a cheeky smile, she loads them onto her tray and goes.

"Hey," the bartender says, rapping his knuckles on the bar like he always does. "Abbi, I'm gonna need another minute on your order. But the new bouncer is asking for you."

"What? Table zero is not in my section." It's always somebody's job to keep the bouncer in free coffee and soda.

He shrugs. "He just came on shift, and asked for you by name. You're very popular tonight. Go take him this?" He sets a glass of Coke on the bar. "Tell him I couldn't add rum. House rules."

Oh good grief. Like I don't have enough to do already. But it would take longer to argue than to deliver the man's soda. I take the drink and head for the vestibule.

On my way, I notice that table fifteen's beers are empty. Better make this quick. I hurry toward the front door, where the bite of winter air chills my skin. "Here's your—"

The sentence dies in my throat when I see who the new bouncer is.

FOURTEEN

NOT GETTING KICKED OUT OF THE
BISCUIT

Weston

"And then Patrick wakes up in the bed with a shiner. And he's
like, *Guys, guys? Who hit me?*" Tate laughs at his own story-
telling. And then he punches me in the arm. "Weston. *Bro*. You
dragged me out here tonight, but you're not a very attentive
date. I'm starting to get offended. Did you even hear what I
said?"

"Yup," I say, turning to face him. "Patrick. Black eye. Got it.
Now we can tell him apart from Paxton."

Tate just shakes his head at me. "Well, at least your hearing
still works. But eyes up here, big guy. If you keep staring at the
hot waitress, she might decide the hockey team is creepy. The
entire wait staff will start bringing us cold chicken and warm
beer."

"Oh, save it." I sip from my excellent beer and fight the
urge to look at Abbi again. I'm so busted.

"I don't think you realize how serious this problem could
be," Tate insists. "If Abbi thinks you're a creeper, we'd have to

find a new hangout. The pizza place, probably. All those carbs, man. We'll get fat and slow."

Vonne snickers. "I like pizza, Weston. I'll make the switch for you if it comes to that."

"What are you *talking* about?" I grumble. "We're not getting kicked out of the Biscuit."

Tate laughs. "I just need to keep your attention for a whole minute. Hudson and I have a bet going." He checks his watch. "Stay with me for at least another thirty seconds, okay? You've got a bad case of ADD. In your case, that stands for Abbi Deficit Disorder."

Everyone at the table laughs, while I roll my eyes. He's right, though. I'm sitting in this bar tonight just hoping to get a smile from Abbi. This crush I have on her just won't be silenced. It's actually worse now, in spite of the fact that she knows all my family's ugly secrets.

We could be so good together. And I think there's still a chance for us. We're not fake dating anymore, right? So if I put Mr. Smooth to work on Abbi, she won't feel cornered. She could just turn me down if she's not feeling it.

But she won't turn me down. I bet she'll invite me back to her place for New Year's Eve with Mr. Smooth. I've got big plans for us.

Sure, it's a little risky, because I want us to stay friends. And she already knows that Mr. Smooth is also Mr. Keep it Casual. But maybe that's just fine with her. Abbi is a busy girl who's juggling a lot in her life. She's going to graduate and move to another city.

But before she does, we could have some fun. Maybe I'm flattering myself, but I think she'd be open to this idea. I'm pretty good at reading people, which is why Mr. Smooth rarely hears the word *no*. One of my talents is knowing when a girl wants me to hit her upvote button.

There was a moment there over Christmas when we were on the same page. Several moments. And now it's eleven thirty on New Year's Eve. It's customary to get a kiss at midnight, right?

All I have to do is get a moment with an overworked waitress in a crowded room. No problemo.

Even as I have this thought, I look up to see Abbi streak by. She stops at a nearby table, clears away the empty beer glasses, nodding vigorously as she takes another order. But there's a new furrow between her eyebrows that's not usually there.

She looks worried.

Huh.

I watch her trot off to the bar. And then I watch her do a hundred other things in the space of ten minutes. She looks frantic. And I know it's not because of the packed tables or the drink orders. Abbi doesn't get overwhelmed at work.

She keeps looking at the door to the bar, though. As if she expects Dracula himself to come through it. And I wish I knew why.

Finally, there's just a few minutes left until midnight. I'm rehearsing my speech in my head. *Listen, Abbi, there's something I need to ask you. And if you say no, I'll never bring it up again.*

This setup does, I realize, come perilously close to my personal rule of never hitting on people who are just trying to make it through a shift at work. But Abbi and I are friends. And I wouldn't go there if I didn't think she was into me.

I slide off my bar stool. "Well guys, wish me luck."

"Oh shit," Hudson says, his eyes big. "Don't crash and burn, man. We'll have to find another hangout. Hell—even if you knock her on her ass with your sex appeal, we're still in trouble."

"How do you figure?" I ask. I'm not really worried, but Hudson is entertaining.

"Dude, you're a heartbreaker," he says. "When you're done with her, she won't bring us beer."

"You know, I don't think that will happen this time."

"Oh God!" Tate moans. "I hope you all like pizza."

"And you guys call yourselves my friends? Here goes nothing."

The music has stopped, and all the bar TVs are tuned in to Times Square. The countdown is just a minute or so away. I dodge between tables, heading for the back, where I last saw Abbi.

Sure enough, she's standing in the shadows near the kitchen door, whispering with the other waitress, Carly. Their heads are bent together in conversation, and then Abbi gestures toward the door.

I hate to interrupt, but I'm a man on a mission. "Hey, ladies."

They both straighten quickly, as if caught out. "Do you need something, Weston?" Abbi asks.

"Oh yeah, he does," Carly snickers. Then she steps around me and makes herself scarce.

"Well, in a manner speaking," I say with a Mr. Smooth chuckle. "You got a minute?"

"For you, of course. But—and this is so embarrassing—I have to ask you a small favor. Another platter of wings kind of favor."

"No problem. Hit me up." I lean against the paneled wall and give her a smile. And then I let my gaze drift to Abbi's pretty mouth. I'd like to own it with mine.

But maybe I'm slipping, because it doesn't erase the crease of worry in Abbi's forehead. "Price is outside. My idiot step-stepbrother." She crosses her arms over her chest. "Remember him?"

"Unfortunately." This is not where I'd hoped to take the

conversation. Behind me, the New Year's revelers begin counting down.

"He seems to have landed a job as a bouncer here. I should never have said that it's an easy job, or that the pay rate was so great." She lets out a heavy breath. "And now he's the guy who's supposed to walk me home? He just told me he was looking forward to it."

"Oh, shit," I breathe.

"Yeah." She crosses her arms. "If you're still here when I get off shift, could you, uh, reprise your award-winning role as my boyfriend? Just this once, as a little reminder."

"Of course," I say immediately. "Anytime, Abbi. Seriously. We're super good at this now, right? It's like rolling off a log."

She gives me a smile that's both sad and grateful. "I can't believe I have to deal with him *here*. The only reason I work here at all was to get away from him."

"I know. Shit. That's terrible."

"FIVE...FOUR...THREE...TWO...ONE...HAPPY NEW YEAR!" screams the entire bar.

Abbi gives her head a shake. "I'm sorry. There's probably somewhere else you'd rather be right now."

Not true. "Hey, Happy New Year. Fuck that guy."

"Fuck him," she says with conviction. "Fuck him sideways."

It's so cute that I can't help but laugh. And then I grab her into a quick, comforting hug.

It's not the New Year's moment that I'd hoped for. But it's pretty good nonetheless.

FIFTEEN

SOMETHING CAME UP

Weston

The boys all look at me expectantly when I get back to the table. "Well?" Tate demands. "How'd it go?"

"Something came up," I say.

"Was it your dick?" Hudson asks with a snicker, and I throw a napkin at him. "Stop, asshole. Abbi needs me to walk her home after her shift. There's a guy who's been bothering her."

"Ah," Tate says. "Could it be a ruse, maybe? Like—walk me home and take off my clothes?"

Sadly, I shake my head. "I've met this troublemaker already. Unfortunately, he's real."

"Bummer," Vonne says.

"But it's probably for the best," Tate points out. "We won't lose our table at the Biscuit."

"You have such little faith in me," I grumble. "I wasn't going to break Abbi's heart."

"That's what you always say, though," Cooper points out. "It's all sunshine until it's not."

I take a sip of my beer and ignore him. I wasn't planning on asking Abbi to marry me, for fuck's sake. I know better than to go down the path of forever. But two college students can have a fling without turning it into an epic story of love and betrayal.

Or, at the very least, they can have a lot of sex and then move several hundred miles apart.

As the new year takes its first tentative baby steps, I sip a beer and wait for Abbi's shift to end. One by one my teammates depart. Tate is the first to go. Then Lex, his phone pressed to his ear, a grin on his face.

The men of the Moo U hockey team don't share my caution around falling in love. Well, maybe Patrick does. But he doesn't leave the bar alone, either. He's found a hookup for the night, as he often does.

Eventually, I'm the last man at table seventeen. Abbi shoots me apologetic looks as she hustles around, finishing her shift. But I'm not going anywhere. Not if Abbi needs me.

"Sorry," she says, appearing without her apron around two a.m. "That took forever."

"Hey, it's okay," I insist. "Let's go." I pull on my jacket, because it's going to be a chilly walk up the hill toward her apartment.

We head outside, and I put on my game face. Protection isn't the point of this exercise, I realize. Abbi could surely figure out how to avoid being alone with Price tonight. Rather, *intimidation* is the purpose of my involvement right now. When we walk outside together, I put a protective arm around her. Luckily Price is standing right outside.

"Hey, remember me?" I ask him, stopping to make my point.

"Nah," the oaf says, scowling.

"Yeah, I bet you'd rather forget." I give him a Mr. Smooth

smile. "My offer still stands, though. Bother her, and you're signing yourself up for a dental bill much higher than whatever they're paying you to stand here and watch the door. It's your call."

Then I walk her home, leaving her on her front porch, where Abbi thanks me profusely. "It's ridiculous that you had to do that. But Price and subtlety don't mix."

"I got that impression."

When I leave her on her doorstep again, we share an awkward goodbye, wishing each other Happy New Year, before I turn and go.

The truth is that I never meant to be Abbi's fake boyfriend for longer than it takes to eat a turkey dinner. But now Price is working regular weekends at the Biscuit. And so—as January rolls on—I consider it my sacred duty to keep up the charade.

And I have to say—it's not a bad life. Over the next couple weeks, Abbi and I have lots of late-night talks as I walk her home. She brings me free wings on the regular. And then there are our lengthy text conversations about hockey, wing flavors, and school.

Honestly, if we could just have sex, all my needs would be met. She's basically perfect.

Abbi keeps telling me that I shouldn't bother to walk her home anymore. That Price isn't threatening enough to warrant all this extra attention. But I don't trust Price, so I keep up the vigil. Some nights I arrive late, have a single beer, and do some homework at the bar while Abbi finishes up her shift.

I like it here. The music is good. And even though my teammates have already gone home for the night, I'm pleasantly tipsy, nursing my last beer and reading a short story for my English class on my phone.

"You really don't have to do this," Abbi says as she swings by to grab Tate's abandoned beer glass off table seventeen. She says it a lot, actually. "I can leave with Carly, or sneak out the back while he's escorting someone else to her car."

"Hey, I know," I say with a shrug. "But I like the Biscuit, and it's easier to read when there aren't hockey players calling me to watch a game on TV. This is like the library for me. But with excellent beer."

And, fine, I'm hung up on Abbi. I'm man enough to admit it. So where else would I rather be?

She gives me a sweet smile and a confused shake of her adorable head. And then she runs off to wipe down another table.

This is my life right now, and I've accepted it. Away games are a problem, though. Two weekends a month I'm on a bus with the team, playing U Mass or Maine.

Luckily, I have friends on the women's hockey team. Women love me almost as much as I love women. So it's really no problem to ask my friend Chrissy to have a drink at the bar until Abbi gets off shift the next weekend, and then walk out with her.

You really didn't have to send a friend to babysit me! comes Abbi's text the next morning. *I'm a big girl. I can look after myself.*

I know that, I quickly reply. *But a good fake boyfriend looks after his fake girlfriend even when he's busy making U Conn cry.*

Nice win, by the way. Your fake girlfriend was super proud. That assist in the third period was extra sexy.

Thank you, baby!

See? We have the best relationship on campus. We have

great chemistry. We're mutually supportive of one another.

Except I haven't been this horny since ninth grade, when Joey Birnbaum showed me how to find porn on my phone. And, sure, I could have hooked up on my road trip. The female hockey fans in Maine appreciate Mr. Smooth almost as much as the ones in Vermont.

But it just wouldn't feel right, you know? Maybe I really should consider a career in Hollywood. I'm better at this acting thing than I'd thought. I've gone and convinced myself that Abbi and I are sexual soulmates. I can't cheat on my soulmate.

So I haven't hooked up at all. In fact, I haven't gotten any action since before Thanksgiving—since the night I'd hoped to hook up with Abbi and then realized why we couldn't.

After that, she was sort of under my skin, I guess. Now I'm looking at the longest dry spell in my adult life. It's hard. I mean that literally. Some nights I can't even concentrate because I'm so pent up. The guys are getting used to the way I space out in the middle of conversations.

Yesterday after practice I was sitting on the bench thinking lustful thoughts about Abbi when I spaced out in the middle of an argument between Pax and Patrick about a new defensive play we're working on.

Coach Garfunkle tried to get my opinion, but I had no idea what they'd been saying. "You okay, son? You look a little unsteady."

"He's just horny," Tate had cracked. "He's got it bad for a girl he can't have. Wait—is there a crystal for that?"

The whole team laughed, but Coach Garfunkle pulled a stone out of his pocket. It was—wait for it—oblong and pointy at the end. Like a rose quartz dick. "This is what you need."

Two dozen hockey players roared their approval. "Really?" Lex Vonne had gasped. "Quartz can make you less horny?"

"Well..." Coach Garfunkle shrugged. "At least it will

remind him that there's something in the world harder than his junk."

Yup, I'm the laughingstock of the team now. But at least there's a good reason for it, and that reason is Abbi. I'm waiting for her at the bar again until she's finally ready to leave the Biscuit.

She eventually arrives at my elbow, her apron and visor missing. She's touched up her lipstick, and now I'm staring at her mouth again, the way a puppy eyes the burger on your plate. Hungrily.

"All right," she says, one hand on her hip. "Let's get on with this charade. Although I'm sure he's got the message by now."

"What charade?" a gruff voice barks at close range.

Fuck. I look up to see Price standing right behind her. "Nobody's talking to you, are they?"

"Asshole," Price growls. "You and this stuck-up bitch can have each other. I wouldn't want your sloppy seconds anyway. She and her mom were just trailer trash."

At the mention of her mom, pain flashes in Abbi's eyes.

"Hey, fucknuts," I growl, my blood suddenly pounding in my ears. "Now you've really done it. Take this outside?"

"No," Abbi gasps, her hand shooting out to grasp my wrist. "Don't get into trouble over *him*. He's not worth it."

Price makes a low chuckle. "Please. Make my day."

I really want to. I could flatten him in seconds. I'm sure of it. But Abbi is begging me with her eyes not to.

Shit. It would feel great to deck him. But I know his type. He'll call the cops and press charges for assault. Coach will lose his mind. I can hear the shouting already.

None of that matters, though. Only the look on Abbi's face right now. It's pleading with me for patience. If I hit Price, I'll make her life more difficult in other ways.

"Okay," I say softly. "Okay, honey."

Now, the trouble with being a great actor is that sometimes you lose yourself in your work. That must be why I lean forward and give Abbi a very gentle kiss on the lips. It's a kiss that says: *your big strong boyfriend listens to you.*

At least it was supposed to say that. But the moment our lips touch, something snaps. I'm not the fake boyfriend anymore. I'm not even Mr. Smooth. I've gone past that and straight on to Mr. Sexy Beast.

And Mr. Sexy Beast is famished. His kiss is firm and full of questions. *Isn't this nice? Can I have a taste? Why haven't we done this before?*

At first, Abbi goes still with surprise. But she gets over her shock in a heartbeat. Two hands quickly grip my jacket. Then she stands up on tiptoes to improve our connection.

I tilt my head and tease the seam of her lips with my tongue. Everything is bliss as Abbi lets out a little moan of longing.

But the sound seems to wake her up. Her eyes fly open again, and she takes a quick step backward. "Wow, I..." She takes a deep breath.

And then we both say "Sorry," at the same time.

Yup. It's awkward.

I look around and see a scowling Price on the far side of the room. He's offering another waitress a walk to her car. And she's turning him down.

Price is an honest-to-god predator. And I can't forget that Abbi only asked for protection from him. She didn't ask for my tongue in her mouth.

Right. Okay. I grab my backpack off the back of the bar stool and gesture for Abbi to precede me out of the Biscuit.

I have got to get a hold of myself. Abbi is a friend who

asked for my help. The least I could do is not maul her like Price.

We walk away from the restaurant and head up the hill toward Abbi's place in silence. I hope I haven't totally fucked things up between us. But I'm not sure how to ask. And we arrive at the creaky front steps of her Victorian building before I work it out.

"So..." She clears her throat as we climb the steps. I always walk her all the way to the door.

"So." I sigh. "Back there, that was..."

"Really great," she says quickly. "Just putting that out there."

Dude, Mr. Smooth whispers into my ear. *You got this.*

"It was, wasn't it?" I smile at her. "And you know what?"

"What?" she squeaks, looking up at me with hope in her eyes.

"The truth is that I'm not a very good actor. Never have been. I'm only convincing when I'm really excited about the role."

"Is that so?"

I don't even answer the question. I take Abbi in my arms instead. And I stare down into her gray eyes as I take her mouth in a firm kiss. She melts against me. *Finally*. This kiss is 100% real. It's the one we've needed since Thanksgiving. Since forever.

Mr. Smooth is nowhere to be found. I don't feel smooth when Abbi's around. There's only the bumbling idiot who needs her so badly. And the Sexy Beast who'll take over when he gets the chance.

And now is his chance. I wrap an arm around Abbi's waist and pull her tightly to my body. Her bag goes *thunk* onto the porch, and her hands grip my jacket.

"Abbi," I say between kisses. "Come home with me."

"No," she says, and I almost weep with disappointment. But then she says, "My place is closer."

Yaaaaaas!

And then we're in motion. I reach down and grab her bag, while she whips a hand inside, fishing for her keys, hurrying to open the outer door then unlock the door to her unit. The moment we step inside her apartment, I lean down and sweep her up into my arms again.

She lets out a little gasp of shock as her feet leave the floor.

"Is this okay?" I ask.

"Hell yes. I was just surprised."

"Good." I kick the door shut and then brace her against it. "Let's get a few things straight before I carry you to bed."

"O-kay," she stammers, wrapping her legs around me.

She can probably feel my cock pressing against her core now. "Look, I've needed to kiss you for a long time. And I don't want to wait any longer." Just to prove my point, I skim my lips along her jaw, and then down her neck. "Is that okay with you?"

"Yes," she says with a shiver and a little groan.

"Good. There's a few more things I need, if it's okay."

"Like what?" she whispers.

"No more acting, honey. I'm handing over my Academy Award. This time I want it to be real." I glance into the shadows of her little one-room apartment. "Is that headboard sturdy?"

"Y-yes..."

Abbi rolls her hips against me, and now it's me who groans. "Aw, yeah. I'm going to need you to moan my name again. But this time, I want to be inside you when you do it."

She swallows roughly. "That can be arranged."

"Good." I sink into another kiss, and her mouth is hot and welcoming.

SIXTEEN
THE SHAPE OF YOU

Abbi

Braced in Weston's strong arms, his taste on my tongue, I'm flooded with several conflicting sensations at once. His chest is warm and solid against mine. His kiss is bossy and loving. Lord knows that nobody ever holds me. I haven't felt so *protected* in a very long time.

God, I'm such a girl. But this man just *threatened* Price for me. If that's not sexy, I don't know what is.

Making a hungry noise, Weston changes the angle of his kiss and then plunders my mouth again. And wow—I didn't know you could feel utterly safe and still super excited at the same time. But here we are. I have no idea what he'll do next, but I already know I'll like it.

"Abbi," he whispers against my mouth. "Did you feel it? On Christmas Eve? I was so hard for you I couldn't sleep. I wanted to roll over and pull you underneath me."

"Oh," is all I can think to say. But that sounds wonderful. Threading my hands into his hair, I kiss him again to show that I agree.

"I need to know," he growls. "Was it just me that night?"

"No," I whisper, licking into his mouth again. I can't believe I'm making out against my door with Weston. *Finally*.

"Did you get hot for me?" His deep voice rumbles in my ear. "Did you get wet?"

"Yes," I admit, as the same thing happens again.

He groans. "Yesterday morning I woke up thinking about you. Had to fuck my hand in the shower just to calm down."

Whew. Is it hot in here? "W-why did we wait so long?"

"Because our lives are complicated. But Abbi—now I'm taking you to *bed*. So if that's not what you want, you gotta speak up right now."

"Yes. Fine. Good."

I sound like a dingus, but Weston doesn't care. He lets out a horny groan and then lifts me off the wall to do exactly what he'd said he would do—he carries me across my small apartment and deposits me on the bed. "I'm going to need you naked."

"Yessir."

Peeling off his jacket, he grunts. "Feel free to say that often. Did you happen to notice that your apartment is cold?"

"Is it?" I toss my jacket aside and kick off my shoes. I don't want to talk about my stupid apartment. I want to get back to the part where he's murmuring dirty words in my ear.

He unbuttons his shirt. And holy Toledo, I get my first full view of the vines tattooed across his chest. They're beautiful. *He's* beautiful. No wonder there's a line of women around table seventeen every time the hockey team racks up a win.

"You're staring," he says with a chuckle.

"Sorry." I avert my eyes.

"No—look all you want. But can you take off your clothes while you're doing it?" He steps closer to me, grips my Biscuit uniform shirt and lifts it over my head. "Now we're talking."

Could he *be* any sexier? From his rippling abs to his chatty, no-nonsense approach to sex, Weston is making me crazy. I find myself staring up at his bare chest again, at those abs that are now prickled with goose bumps. "You're cold," I say softly.

"Abbi, it's like the Polar Vortex in here. Get under the covers with me. I'll keep us both warm."

Now that's an excellent plan. I hop off the bed and turn down the covers, including the down comforter I had to buy when I realized that the landlady was never going to turn up the heat.

Weston doesn't waste any more time, either. I hear the sound of a zipper's metal teeth as he sheds his jeans. I turn away to undo the hook on my skirt, so I miss the view of Weston's naked body sliding into my bed. By the time I step out of my skirt, he's already covered himself.

Still—here's a sight I never thought I'd see—Weston Griggs in my bed, his hands folded behind his head, biceps flexing on my pillow.

Pinch me.

His eyes are smiling up at me. "Get in here before you freeze. Right here, baby." He lifts one side of the covers. Still wearing my bra and panties, I slip into the bed beside him.

Weston turns and rolls until he's spread out above me, his warm body pressing me against the mattress. And—hello—there's a very hefty erection pressed against my thigh.

Holy heck. This just got real.

"Now *this* is where I wanted you on Christmas Eve, Abbi. And on Thanksgiving, and New Year's. And every night in between." He strokes a thumb across my cheekbone. "We are going to have *all* the sex."

I giggle nervously. It's been a while for me. My life is too chaotic for fun and hookups.

And Weston is a player. Even though I haven't seen him pick up anyone in the bar in a while, I know how much he likes women. I hope he isn't expecting me to be a sex goddess or something. I hope I don't smell like chicken wings and beer. And—wait—did I shave my legs today? At least these sheets are clean.

"Hey. Abbi," he whispers, kissing the bridge of my nose. "Where did you go just now?"

"I'm here!" I say breathlessly. "We were just about to have all the sex—" I actually bite my tongue in an effort to stop rambling. Ow. "Sorry. Just a brief moment of performance anxiety."

"Do we have to sing it out?" His pretty eyes smile down at me. "Should I cue up a song on my phone?"

"What?" I snort in an unsexy way. "No! Oh my God."

"Hang on. Maybe I'm on to something." He grins. "Which song would be most appropriate for this? How about 'Shape of You' by Ed Sheeran? It's about a bar hookup. I don't know if I can sing that high, though."

"Weston!" I clap a hand over my mouth to keep from laughing in his face.

"There's always the classic—'Let's Get it On.'" Weston props himself up on an elbow and looks thoughtful. "Or Bruce singing 'I'm on Fire.' But I think I prefer The Kinks. 'You Really Got Me' speaks the truth. Because I can't sleep at night, either."

I blink up into his handsome face, and wonder if he's even serious. Then he puts those sexy lips together and slowly hums the Kinks' guitar riff. And I forget that he's making a joke as that sexy mouth descends to the swell of my breast, tracing my curves very slowly, his hum vibrating across my skin.

Whoa. Now I've got goose bumps, and not because of the

cold. As he teases my breast, I forget to be nervous. I even forget to breathe. The tickle and scrape. The heat of his mouth...

Wow.

My bra is in the way, though. Reaching back, I unhook that sucker.

"Good girl," Weston breathes. He grabs the bra and tosses it away. "Fuck, Abbi." He brings one roughened hand to my breast and gives me a gentle squeeze. "So pretty." Then he lowers his mouth to my nipple, glancing up at me as he extends his tongue to lap at my peak.

And I let out a hot gasp of excitement. Playful, dirty Weston does not disappoint. He closes his lips around my nipple and sucks. Then he pops off to torture the other breast. And all the while he watches me with those bright, curious eyes.

Is this real life? I feel *worshipped*. My hands find his muscular shoulders, and I slide my fingers all over his beautiful skin, tracing the vines of those tattoos.

But then he disappears from view, under the covers. "Weston," I cry, my hands seeking him under the sheet. "Where did you—?"

Two hands tug my underwear off. Then his broad hands land on my thighs, and lips begin to trace and kiss the curve of my hip bone.

Oh boy. I lift the edge of the comforter and peek, because this is too incredible to miss.

As I illuminate Weston, a muffled *"whoa"* comes from under the covers. He lifts his head. "Who's a bad girl, Abbi? Do you have a tattoo of a black lab on your thigh?"

"That's Friendly."

"Oh, I can be very friendly," he says with a grin. "But who's the dog?"

"No, I mean the dog was *named* Friendly. She was my first pet."

He laughs. "Kidding, honey. I got it the first time." He presses a palm down over my tattoo. "Don't watch, doggo. I'm about to go down on your master."

I moan. "The things that come out of your mouth."

"Yeah, I don't think you mind 'em too much." Weston gives me a sexy wink—an actual wink—and then he lowers his mouth to my—

Oh God. "Oh GOD." That tongue. He's shameless. It's a struggle to relax against the bed as he licks and kisses me. My toes curl, and my hips roll. It's so good. Nobody has ever lavished so much attention on me.

Never. Ever.

I just hope I'm not too sad when it's over.

SEVENTEEN

I FEEL LIKE A SUPERHERO

Weston

Mr. Smooth has fled the building again. And the way I feel right now, I don't even remember the sound of his voice. All that's left is this babbling, crazy guy who can't calm down.

Who could blame me? There's a goddess spread out in front of me, every curve ripe for touching and teasing. I'm driving her wild, and I feel like a superhero. If the superhero were a super horny college guy who's fallen deeply in like with his fake girlfriend.

I tease my thumb in a slow circle around her clit and try not to hump the bed. I feel loose and wild tonight. Part of it is pent-up sexual desire. I've been waiting a long time for this moment to arrive.

But I'm weirdly nervous, too. I want to please her so badly.

"Omigod *Weston!*" Abbi pants, clutching my hair.

"Is there something you want?" I tease, sliding a finger inside.

She moans.

Jesus Christ, I'm so revved up. Who knew that a bit of a dry spell could ruin a man's restraint?

Crawling back up her body, I grab for the condom I'd retrieved from my jacket as I got undressed. I roll it on while she watches with big, hungry eyes.

I'm a good lover. A confident, generous lay. *Usually*. Right now I feel like a nervous teenager on prom night. This is momentous. It's big. And I'm not referring to Little Mr. Smooth, although he's harder than ever.

It's because Abbi and I are such close friends, right? That must be why my heart is thumping like a kick drum right now. I care about her happiness, because I'm a good friend.

These are the thoughts bouncing around in my stunned head as I melt back down onto Abbi's supple body. I drop kisses on her shoulders. On her neck. Wherever I want. And that's a lot of places, apparently. I can't believe that I'm finally allowed to drag my lips across her flat belly, and then suck lightly on the tips of her dusky nipples.

God, I'm so hungry for her. And it must be mutual, because Abbi spreads her legs in invitation. "Please," she whispers. "You know you want to."

I let out a helpless groan, because she isn't wrong. Then I grab the base of my cock and squeeze tightly, trying to calm myself down. Usually the tight grip of the condom does the trick, but tonight all bets are off.

Come on, Mr. Smooth! Why has he deserted me at this crucial hour?

I give Abbi a confident smile nonetheless. Then I slide right into her tight heat. It feels so good that I close my eyes momentarily, just to appreciate the sensation of our joining.

"Oh yessss," she breathes. Her silky hands find my chest, and she wraps her legs possessively around my ass.

My eyes flip open to find hers watching me. She looks

breathless and a little stunned, which is just how I feel too. "Wow," I say stupidly. It's pretty much the only thought in my brain at this point.

"This is definitely the best idea I've ever had," she whispers.

"Oh, so it was your idea?" I ask, rolling my hips provocatively. "News flash, my dick thinks about this all the time."

She grips my shoulders and moves against me. "He should have made his wishes known. You were going to leave me on the front porch tonight."

"Fair," I say, giving her a slow thrust. "He's learned his lesson."

She smiles, and I lean down and kiss her deeply. I'm so turned on that I have to proceed with caution. It's time to think about hockey practice. Drills. Conditioning. Boring sessions on the treadmill...

Abbi purrs beneath me. She runs her foot up and down the back of my leg. I kiss her as deeply as I dare while we slowly move together in the age-old dance. I wasn't kidding when I'd said I dreamed of pulling her underneath me. The way she gazes up at me with soft eyes is just perfect.

Too perfect, actually. After a while I roll over, pulling her on top of me. This small break in the action calms me down. And the view is *wow*. Abbi blinks down at me with mussed hair and luscious, swaying breasts. "You are so fucking hot," I whisper. "And I am really fucking close. Ride me."

"Okay," she breathes.

"Put your hands on the headboard."

"Like this?" She leans forward and grips the bed above me.

"Exactly like that." I reach back and slap her ass. "Go on."

She lets out a deep, sexy breath and begins to move. And I'm in paradise as she slowly picks up the pace. I'm watching for that perfect moment when she finds the rhythm that makes her body sing. And when it happens, it's beautiful. Her head drops as she sounds out a little breathy moan on every stroke.

"There, baby," I say through a clenched jaw. "Give it to me." I cup both of her tits, which bounce in my hands, and she moans more loudly. Then I skim my fingertips down her belly and right to the place of our joining.

"*Fuck*, Weston," she groans happily. "*Yes yessssss.*"

Then I can't hold back anymore. My balls get impossibly tight and I groan from the effort of staving it off. But it's no use. I jack my hips off the bed and bounce her on my cock. The headboard begins to bang rhythmically into the wall, and I gasp as my climax hits me full force.

God almighty it's a doozy. Grabbing her by the hips, I let out a growl of sheer relief. And then a shout of joy. I catch Abbi in my arms as she lets go of the headboard and drops onto my body with a deep, satisfied moan. And I feel her body pulse deliciously around mine.

We end up as a pile of limbs and heavy breathing. And I have never been so satisfied in my life.

That blissed-out feeling doesn't go away, either. Usually, after a hookup, I wait around a little while and then head home. That's my MO. It sends a friendly message but promises nothing.

Tonight is different. I don't want to leave this bed, and Abbi's warm body. I don't want to leave, period. We just had amazing sex. Like, Division One championship sex. I think it broke my brain. All I want to do is hold her and nuzzle her neck.

"Okay if I stay?" I ask eventually. "It's kinda late and kinda cold outside."

"You can stay," she whispers, palming my heart.

"Thanks, Abbi." We blink at each other, but nobody moves for another moment. She's so easy to be around. If I were looking for a real girlfriend, I'd look for one exactly like her.

She's the one who breaks our staring contest. "One sec. Let me find you a toothbrush."

We take turns in Abbi's frigid bathroom. Then we slide into her bed together one more time and pull up the comforter that we'd kicked off the bed during our sexcapades.

"Night, hot stuff," I say from my side of the bed.

"Night, Westie," she yawns.

And then I fall deeply asleep, before I can decide whether I actually like that silly name or not.

In the morning, I wake up to the sound of her alarm.

"What time is it?" I croak, my hand somehow curled against her hip. My nose at the back of her neck. This is so unusual for me. I haven't woken up pressed against a woman in a really long time.

It's nicer than I remember.

"Eight," she whispers, her fingers trailing over my hand.

"You have somewhere you need to be?"

"No."

"Good," I grunt. Then I roll her, pulling her warm body onto my chest.

Ooh, a naked woman, Mr. Smooth says.

But for once I ignore him, and we sleep a while longer.

The next time I wake up, we're cuddled together like we've been sharing a bed for years. I can tell she's awake, so I run a hand down her arm. "Your skin is cold," I whisper. "Is it always this cold in here?"

"Yes," she says. "Although I didn't notice it much last night."

I chuckle and then kiss her shoulder. "Last night was epic."

"Yes it was," she agrees softly.

"Do you, uh…" I realize too late that I haven't planned what I was going to say. And I'm in uncharted territory here. "Do you think we'll end up doing it again sometime?" *Right now works for me*, I almost add.

"That sounds glorious," she says carefully. "But I just assumed you didn't do repeats."

Well, ouch. Hearing my own behavior reflected back at me shuts me up for a second. She's right, but I didn't know it was so obvious.

"I didn't mean it as a criticism," she says into the silence. "I promise."

"No—I know you didn't. But you and I are friends, right? And we'll stay that way?"

"Of course." She gives me a tentative glance.

I curl an arm around her, and tuck her cheek onto my bare shoulder. "You already know why I don't do relationships."

"You mean because your family is an advertisement for love gone wrong? Or because it's more fun to party your way through the female hockey fans of Vermont?"

I snort, although it's hard to argue with this assessment. "I meant the first thing. But I'm not ashamed of the second."

She reaches an arm up and ruffles the hair above my ear. "You shouldn't be ashamed. I'm just envious of your fun."

"We had a lot of fun last night, right?"

"We set the *standard* for fun," she agrees. "In the dictionary now there's a picture of our clothes on the floor."

"Agreed," I say, "And only because Merriam-Webster would never print a photo of the best parts of last night." I run a hand down her bare ass and squeeze. "But that's why I think

—since we're both reasonable adults who enjoy our fun—we could just keep the party going. What do you say to that? It would be our special arrangement for fun."

"Like friends with benefits?" she asks.

"Exactly like that. This would be casual. You're graduating in the spring, anyway. So our fun already has a sell-by date."

"You're right," she murmurs. "It totally does."

"And there's a bonus—your idiot step-stepbrother will see me waiting for you to get off work." My voice drops in pitch as I stroke her smooth belly with my happy fingers. "I won't even be acting."

She laughs. "Okay, sure. But he got the message already, I think."

"He'd better have." God, how I still want to punch that guy.

Abbi finally rolls over to study me with her clear gray eyes. "Just because I don't think I need your help anymore with the Price thing doesn't mean I don't appreciate it. Thank you for standing up for me. It's been really nice of you."

"Anytime," I say, my voice husky. And that's when my phone alarm finally goes off. "Oh, hell. I guess it's nine thirty already."

"I should get up, too," Abbi says, sitting up.

Our perfect night is ending, and I'm just not ready. "Should we shower together? And then I can take you out for bagels and a vat of hot coffee. Just to take off the chill in your room. How do you even get out of bed in the morning?"

She smiles down at me. "That sounds nice, and I won't turn you down. But I do have a system for this. That robe"—she points at a flannel bathrobe over a nearby chair—"is strategically positioned so that I can reach it from the bed." She leans toward the chair, yanking the robe onto her bed. "Extra layers are the only way to get out of this bed when it's so cold in here."

I put a hand on the soft flannel. "This is nice. Is it from that place where you have your internship?"

"Yes. My employee discount is super handy."

"Will we both fit inside this robe?"

"No." She giggles. "But I'll turn on the water and call you when it's warm."

"Good plan."

EIGHTEEN
PINCH ME

Abbi

Weston Griggs is naked in my shower.

Naked. In *my* shower.

Pinch me!

Getting clean has never been so much fun. We don't fool around, except for a few kisses. But Weston makes a point of soaping up my back—and my ass. And when I wash his hair he makes appreciative noises and then kisses my neck.

It's the most fun I've ever had on a school day. And I'm sad to leave the warm embrace behind—both Weston's and the hot water. But we both have things to do. So I pass him a clean towel.

It ought to feel super strange moving around my tiny apartment with a ripped, naked Weston. But the boy is so comfortable with himself and so goofy that it just doesn't feel awkward.

I'm starting to think that some of his good-natured cheer is a coping mechanism, though. He probably isn't the world's happiest human. He's just learned to find the light-hearted, funny thing in every situation and cling tightly to it.

There are worse traits in a human. I admire him for trying.

"Okay, who can you call to turn up the heat in your apartment?" he asks as we dry off and dress. "Not that I mind the view. It's very nipply in here," he says, eyeing my breasts through the bra I'm trying to straighten. "Maybe that's your landlord's play."

"Doubt it. The landlady is a super-cheap octogenarian. She lives on this floor, in a unit at the back of the building. Twice I've slipped notes under her door asking for her to turn up the temperature. When that didn't work, I mailed her a formal request. She never answered. I'm afraid to piss her off too badly. And I only need to live here until May, right?"

"Yeah, but I hate to let the old bat refrigerate you," Weston presses. "Isn't there a thermostat you could fiddle with?"

"The controls must be in her apartment. In my apartment, there's only this metal thing that looks somewhat important. But there's no way to control it." I point toward the kitchen, where a dull gray metal rectangle is surrounded by a small metal cage high on the wall.

Weston walks over and stares up at it. "That's got to be *some* part of the heat and hot water system," he agrees. "And you'd never put a valve that far off the ground."

"Okay..." I don't know why he's so interested. "Do you have a plumbing kink I should know about?"

"Baby, *plumbing* is very sexy." He gives me a cheesy Weston wink. "But I'm an architect's kid. I've heard a lot of dinner table discussion about heating. And that might be a thermostat."

"There aren't any controls on it. I climbed up on the counter once and checked."

"Let's just try something. Do you have a spare dish towel or a washcloth?"

"Sure." I go back into the bathroom and find him a washcloth. "What for?"

He takes it from me and wets it in the kitchen sink. Then he wrings it out. "This will cause evaporation," he explains, "which will trick the thermostat into thinking that your apartment is even colder than it actually is." As I watch, he tosses the wet cloth up until it lands on the cage.

And then it promptly slides off again, hitting my floor with a wet slap.

"Huh. Do you have a chair I could stand on?"

"I got it," I say, walking over to my tiny counter and putting the loaf of bread on top of the drying rack to make a space. Give me a hand?"

Weston makes a sling out of his hands, and I step onto it. A minute later I'm standing on the counter. Weston hands me the cloth and I spread it out over the cage. "What are the chances this will make a difference?"

"Pretty high," he says. "I think you'll come home to a warm apartment. You'll just have to reset the wet towel when you're cold. Now let's go eat bagels. I'm starved."

Weston is magic. And I don't mean the sex. When I return to my apartment after my morning classes, the place is *toasty*. It's mind blowing. I don't have to freeze anymore, and for a couple of days, the change is a little hard to get used to.

So is Weston, if I'm honest. I'm not accustomed to receiving sexy texts from him in the middle of my day. Or a voice message asking me if I'm okay to walk home after work the next night.

Price only works on the weekends, I remind him. *I'm good.*

Yes you are, Weston replies, and I blush at my phone. *And I should really stay in and study for this test in statistics. But I'd rather walk you home again.* He follows that up with a wink emoji.

Pinch me. This can't be my real life.

I have a lot of studying to do too, I admit. *And I'm working the next four nights.*

Nooooooo, he types back. *I have back-to-back games out of town this weekend.* He follows that up with a pouting emoji. *Is there any chance you're free Sunday night?*

I am totally free on Sunday night, I reply quickly.

Phew. Let's have dinner together after I get back to town. I owe you from our bet.

I blink down at this lovely invitation and try not to dance around like a lunatic. *I'd love to,* I reply instead.

"What is that look on your face?"

I jump at the sound of Carly's voice, and I shove my phone into my back pocket. "Just texting with, um, Weston."

Carly lets out a shriek. "Omigod! I knew it! He's in lovvvve with you!"

"Shhh!" I hiss. "You're wrong. We're just having…" I struggle for words, because this thing with Weston is as hard to explain as it is to believe. "A thing."

"A thing…" Carly repeats slowly as she shoves a soda glass against the dispenser and fills it with Coke. "Like a *relationship?*" There are hearts in her eyes already.

"God no. A fling. A tryst. A convenient arrangement."

"So you're not 'just friends' anymore."

"Yes we are," I insist. We're just friends who—" I don't finish the sentence, because Kippy is somewhere nearby and I don't want to be overheard.

"Oh my *God,* this is the most exciting thing I've heard in a *long* time. And speaking of long things...is his thing long?" She giggles.

"Stop it," I hiss. "That's an inappropriate question."

She lets out a dreamy sigh. "Fine. But what about his stamina. I'll bet an athlete like that can go all night."

I snort. "There will be no details given out."

"Whyyyy?" she whines. "It's not like I'll ever find out for myself. Weston is going to fall for that cute, sassy thing you've got going on. You just took him off the market. And they said it couldn't be done."

"It's just temporary," I insist. "This is just a physical thing until we both move on. I'll be leaving Vermont before June, you know."

"Still," Carly says. "A girl could have a lot of terrific sex in four months. Come on! Just give me one detail."

I bite my lip, gather up four ketchup bottles and carry them away. I will not gossip about Weston to Carly. Even though I am impressed. And I can say with certainty that hockey players do possess an awful lot of stamina.

"You have a dreamy look on your face," Carly says with a snicker. "Are you seeing him again tonight?"

"No," I say. "We're going out to dinner on Sunday. So nobody had better ask me to work a shift."

"If he's taking you out, that sounds like a relationship!"

"We're settling up a bet," I insist. "Stop using that word, Carly. Weston doesn't do relationships."

"He hasn't *yet*," she argues. "You could be his first."

"It's never happening," I tell the both of us. Because I'm not dumb enough to fall in love with him.

Thank goodness for that.

NINETEEN

MAKE IT A GOOD ONE

Weston

I'm waiting outside of El Cortijo—a kickass little restaurant downtown on Bank Street—and practically tapping my toe with impatience.

Abbi isn't late. But after a long week, I'm just really looking forward to seeing her again, and having excellent Mexican food.

And, fine, excellent sex. I've been buzzing ever since our night together, and I need a repeat. Now, preferably.

I've spent the last couple of days thinking about Abbi. Actually, that's the polite way of putting it. It would be more accurate to say that I spent most of my waking hours remembering how good it was to finally spread her out and love her up like I'd been wanting to for months now.

And now I'm hooked. I can't stop thinking about it, or planning our next naked adventure. Here stands a desperate man, hungry for both tacos and sweet, sweet satisfaction.

"Weston!" I swing around to see her trotting down the

sidewalk toward me, a hat perched on her head, her cheeks pink from the cold. "Were you waiting long?"

"Nope," I say, lunging for her. I pull her in and kiss her hello. *Very* firmly.

She wraps her arms around me and gives it right back. But then she breaks off the kiss before I'm ready. "Well hello, sailor. How was the war?"

"Just been, um, waiting to do that." I give her a big smile. Then I grab the door handle and usher her inside. "Have you been here before?"

"No." She shakes her head. "It's so cute."

It is, I guess. The restaurant is in one of those old metal diner cars from the fifties. There's counter seating on the right, and a single row of booths stretching the length of the left side.

Luckily, there's a spot open in the middle, and a waitress shows us to the table and puts down two paper placemats. "Can I start you off with some drinks? Beer? Sangria? Margarita?"

Abbi's eyes light up. "I'd love a margarita. On the rocks, no salt. Thanks!"

I order a beer, and then watch as Abbi scans the menu. "God, this looks great."

"It is." I chose this place because it's casual. The food is amazing here, but it isn't date-night fancy. I didn't want to make a big statement, you know?

Just a casual dinner between friends.

Friends who are definitely getting lucky later. If I have anything to say about it.

"What's your usual order?" Abbi wants to know.

"The lengua tacos. Oh, and we have to get some guacamole. This is my treat, by the way. Because you won our bet."

140

"Yum. This *is* a treat. Although I'm not convinced I won this bet, Westie."

The nickname makes me smirk. "You absolutely did. Besides, I was in the mood for Mexican." I am also in the mood for Abbi, who's happily perusing the specials on a card taped to the napkin dispenser.

When the waitress comes back a few minutes later, Abbi actually giggles as the frosty margarita lands in front of her. "Someone else bringing me a drink! This is awesome."

Well, hell. Now I want to bring her all the drinks. "So how's the job search going?" I ask after the waitress takes our order.

"It's…going," she says, propping her cheek in her hand. "I have two interviews coming up in New York, one at a big clothing brand, and one at a bank. But one of the jobs is in social media."

"That's not good?"

She fingers her silverware. "It *could* be good. I realize that everyone starts somewhere. But some of these brands are so big that they have a stable of young women who *only* do social media. It's a game of likes and clicks. But there's no way to advance. And when you can't stand it anymore, you quit and they just find another fresh-faced grad."

"So you'll keep looking," I say.

"I'm going to try. I have a lead on a job at a mortgage bank, too. That's the opposite situation—it's all interest rates and credit checks and building the loan portfolio."

"That sounds…"

"Dry," she prompts. "It's okay, you can say it. Maybe I have to pay my dues somewhere boring. I still need a paycheck and a foot in the door somewhere. And if I pick something in a major city, at least I'll be locating myself in a decent job market."

"You'll get there." I sound like a damn cheerleader. But I

mean it. Who wouldn't want Abbi on their team? "Someone will appreciate you for more than chicken wings and beer."

"God, I hope so."

"You'll probably get a good recommendation from the flannel people, right?"

"Oh, definitely. In fact, they've asked me to come in for a few hours tomorrow."

"Weren't you done with that internship?"

"I was. But now they want to pay me fifteen bucks an hour to straighten out the *new* intern. It sounds like she's super clueless. She keeps posting rectangular images in the company Instagram feed."

"Oh the horror."

Abbi grins. "The flannel people are so confused. They don't know what to do with a millennial who can't handle social media. It's like a duck who refuses to quack."

I crack up. "Any chance the flannel people will offer you a job?"

Her eyes meet mine as she shakes her head. "It's a family business. They could be so much more if they tried, you know? The quality is there. But they've been making the same product line for fifty years. Besides—guess what they wanted from me as an intern?"

"Social media?"

She makes her fingers into a gun and shoots me. "You got it. And only social media. They see me coming with my marketing degree—and barely old enough to legally drink a margarita—and they're like, *here is our TikTok account. Please do whatever it is that TikTok is for.*"

I snort. "And did you light up TikTok for them?"

"You know it. I dressed up the owner's dog in flannel and got three million views."

"*Three million?*" I yelp.

"It's a really cute dog," she says from over the rim of her margarita glass. "And it's really nice flannel."

"But no wonder companies want you to do social media, babe. You're good at it."

The compliment makes her blush. "I probably just got lucky. But enough about dogs in PJs. What's up with you?"

"First, a big test in organic chemistry. That's going to take some work. And then back-to-back games against Notre Dame."

"You fly there, right?"

"Thank God. It's too far for a bus ride. And we always play both the season's games on the same weekend."

"Are road trips fun?" she asks me.

"Totally fun. But Sunday night is always a doozy for me. It's hard to catch up."

She tilts her head and studies me. "It's Sunday night right now. Should you be studying?"

"No," I insist. "I've been looking forward to seeing you all week." Things like that don't usually fall out of my mouth. I don't like to give anyone the wrong idea.

It is, however, true.

I see another stain of pink hit her cheeks. But she doesn't engage the topic any further. "I'll bet not many hockey players are premed. They don't work as hard at the academics as you."

"Some don't," I admit. "Next year when I'm trying to write med school applications during hockey, it's going to be hell."

"Where do you want to go to grad school?"

"Here, actually. Burlington's program is pretty good. I'm close to my crazy family, but not *too* close. And there's the possibility that I could use my fifth year of NCAA eligibility. I was injured my sophomore year and didn't play."

"Oh! So you could play hockey in grad school?"

"Yeah, or maybe do some coaching if I can't make the

schedule work. Coach has been building this team so well the last couple of years. Great things are coming, and I want to see it play out."

"That's fun, Westie." She gives me a bright smile. "Table seventeen wouldn't be the same without your leadership."

I nudge her feet under the table. "You're trolling me."

"Just a little. Someone else will have to serve the beer, though. I'll be too busy running the world."

"Or at least the world's TikTok account," I point out.

"Exactly," she says with a grin.

After dinner, I hold her hand as we walk back toward campus. The night is frigid, and we have January air blasting in our faces. "I guess I didn't think this through."

"We're from Vermont, Westie." She squeezes my hand. "We can take it."

"If you need warming up, though, I'm volunteering."

She snickers. "Maybe you *did* think this through."

"Not to brag, but I don't usually have to freeze a woman to get her into bed."

Abbi gives me a sly glance. "Is that where the night is headed?"

"It is if I get to choose. Can I come over?" *Please say yes*. I've got it so bad.

"Yes," she says softly.

"If tonight isn't good timing, I'd understand. I know it's your only night off."

"No, it's nice," she says sounding a little shy. "I'd like to spend my night off with you."

Something warm and delicious curls through my belly when I hear this. "My place? Or yours."

"Mine," she says. "It's closer. And more, uh, private."

"That's certainly true. Your place it is." I hitch my gym bag up on my shoulder and lengthen my stride toward her little apartment.

"See?" she says when we finally arrive inside. "It's warm! And I only have you to thank."

"Holy cow," I crow as the heat hits my cold face. "It's actually hot in here. I've created a monster."

"Well, your system of tricking the thermostat is awesome, but it isn't easy to fine tune." She hangs up her coat on the back of the door before crossing the room to pick up a broom. She uses the stick to knock the washcloth off the thermostat.

"I'm glad you're not freezing anymore." I take off my coat and hang it up with Abbi's. "Plus, this is going to make it a lot easier to get you naked. Am I right?" I give her a sleazy wink.

"You might be," she says shyly. "Want a soda?" She taps her fingers against the countertop in her tiny kitchen.

"Only if you do." She looks a little shy all of a sudden. I hope that doesn't mean she's having second thoughts about us.

I *really* hope not.

Then I glance around her apartment and notice something. "You did some redecorating?"

She gives a shrug. "A little. It was cluttered before."

"But now it's *pristine*." The desk is tidy. The bookshelf is straightened. The kitchen is spotless. And the bed is made up crisply, with the pillows perfectly aligned side by side. "Do you clean a lot? Does it help you clear your head?"

"Sometimes," she mumbles, her gaze on her shoes.

"Or, and maybe I'm out of line, here..." I stalk across the room and cup her chin until she looks up at me with guilty eyes. "You cleaned because you thought I might come over tonight?"

"There might be some truth to that." She bites her lip.

"Were you hoping so?" I ask in a low voice.

"Yes."

"Then why are you shy now?" I whisper, my thumb tracing a slow arc across her smooth cheek. "Because I don't feel shy at all right now. I feel like peeling you out of these clothes and reminding you how much fun we had the other night."

She puts a hand in the center of my chest, "Because you're so…"

"So…?" I wait.

Abbi blushes. "So fun. So *extra*. And I usually fall asleep on my textbooks, smelling like chicken wings."

"Well, I do love chicken wings," I tease, moving in closer. "We should be fine."

She gives me a wan smile. "Maybe I just forgot how this works."

"Just kiss me already," I whisper. "And I'll remind you. I promise."

Her gray eyes blink up at me, and that blush grows deeper.

"I'm waiting, Abbi. Make it a good one. Set the tone. You'd be surprised what a good kiss can—"

She shuts me up with soft lips that firm up against mine.

Fuck yes. I catch her in both arms and pull her against my hungry body. She makes a soft little whimper, and that sound slices through me like lightning across a summer sky.

This is just what I've been craving. More of Abbi's kisses. More of her silken hair between my fingers. More more *more*.

I slide my hands down over her sweet ass and then lift her onto that counter. There. Now I can own her mouth without bending down. Now I can sink into her kiss with abandon. And never stop.

TWENTY

MAYBE I DON'T NEED TO KNOW

Abbi

"Wow." It's the first coherent thing I've said in an hour.

I lay panting on my bed, Weston's body—naked and spent —sprawled out diagonally across mine. He's trying to catch his breath.

My mind is blown. So this is what it means to have fantastic sex. It means Weston and me making out on the kitchen counter until I thought I would burst from desire. It means letting him strip off my clothes and spread me out on the bed.

It means yanking down his briefs and taking him into my mouth, while he curses and praises me, sometimes in the same breath. It means watching him suit up in a condom before prowling back to me on hands and knees, a determined look in his eye, while his shoulder muscles pop and flex.

And—this is the part that's so confusing to me—it means undulating beneath him while he stares into my eyes as he kisses me more deeply with every stroke.

Weston's skills are unparalleled. But that's not even the

shocking part. The *intimacy* is. I don't know what to do with all that eye contact. And the broken sounds he makes when he comes.

My poor little lonely heart can't handle all that loving attention. It's like standing too close to a bonfire. You already know how cold you'll feel when you finally step away.

"Abbi," Weston rasps. "Can I stay over?"

"Of course," I say just a little too quickly. "I might even have an extra toothbrush."

"I brought mine," he says with a grin.

"Look who planned ahead," I tease, although my heart is still fluttering over the idea that Weston wants to sleep in my bed tonight.

"I didn't *expect* you to invite me in," he says. "But I sure hoped you would. It's a fine line."

"We could watch a movie or something," I suggest.

"Or something," he whispers.

And I smile up at my ceiling.

Following our Sunday night (and Monday morning!) sexfest, both Weston and I have very busy weeks.

I glimpse him once, on Wednesday night at the Biscuit, but table seventeen is not in my section.

Then, when I'm waiting for an order in the kitchen, I feel my phone buzz with a text. When I pull it out of my pocket, I see the text is from Weston. *I know you're busy. But won't you come over here and give me a kiss?*

Me: *In front of the bitchy manager who will soon owe me a $1500 bonus? Think again.*

Weston: *Bummer. You look hot and I miss you.*

Me: *Never knew you had an apron kink.*

Weston: *I have an Abbi kink. And tomorrow I'm going to South Bend, Indiana. Before we leave, I need to write a paper. So I can't even invite myself over tonight.*

Me: *That is a bummer.*

Weston: *We get back Sunday night. Come over?*

"Ooooh!" Carly shrieks.

I whirl around, and find her reading over my shoulder. "You just about gave me a heart attack."

"I'd have a heart attack too if Weston Griggs invited me over."

"Girls," Kippy says from the doorway. "What's going on?"

I shove my phone into my pocket and grab two plates of wings off the counter. "Not a thing. Excuse me." I lift my chin and march toward the dining room.

"Don't chase after the boys at table seventeen," he says with a sniff. "Be a shame if I had to fire you before your year was out."

Carly lets out an angry gasp, but I don't even break my stride. I carry the wings out and then run a new order to the bar.

And I don't touch my phone for the rest of the night. I can't afford to screw up, no matter how good a kisser Weston is. He's a great guy. I've got only good things to say about him.

He's fun, and he's sexy. But he's a distraction I can't really afford. And that's just the way it is.

On Thursday I dress in the best clothes I own and get on a JetBlue flight to New York City. I'm giving up a shift at work, three classes, and three hundred of my hard-earned dollars to do a few job interviews.

The investment bank where I'm interviewing for a spot in

the training program paid for the plane ticket, but in order to stretch my time in the city, I'm springing for a one-night stay in a hotel.

If I get any of these jobs, it will all be worth it.

Or not. Because the investment bank interviewing process is a stressful whirlwind. I'm herded around the building with at least a dozen other candidates—mostly men. It's completely intimidating. Their crisp navy suits and silk ties make me feel like a country bunny in my sky-blue blazer.

The jacket had belonged to my mother. The tag says Lilly Pulitzer, which is a fancy brand, right? I'd saved it because she'd really liked the color. But I can see now that it's all wrong for this shimmering glass building, where everyone is wearing black, navy, or gray.

There's also a timed math test, which I take in a conference room, hurrying to finish amid the frantic scribbling of other candidates. The guy next to me is a mouth-breather. It's throwing me off my game. I don't get to answer the last question before the proctor says, "Pencils down."

The test is followed by a round of "flash interviews." It's like speed dating, with higher stakes and in uncomfortable shoes.

I paste on a grin and greet the next interviewer. He introduces himself with: "So, Abbi Stoddard, tell me why you deserve to beat out hundreds of other candidates for this job."

Hundreds?

The beat of silence that falls between us for a moment probably tells him more than my eventual answer ever will.

Eight hours later, I've survived both the investment bank and the mortgage bank interview gauntlets. I've also walked forty blocks in heels I borrowed from Carly, rolling my suitcase behind me, just so I could save cab money, and found a decently cheap restaurant in the process.

Now, finally approaching the hotel that I'd booked, I'm full of Chinese food but low on energy. I turn to the left and check for traffic before stepping off the curb.

But then a blur in my peripheral vision has me leaping back just in time to avoid a bicycle coming from the opposite direction.

The guy swerves and brakes. "Hey! Watch it!" he yells over his shoulder before riding away.

Okay, that was *really* close. Too close.

My heart is pounding in my chest, and the *Walk* sign turns back to *Don't Walk* before I'm brave enough to try again.

Now I realize that Seventh Avenue is a one-way street. I should have looked to the right, not the left. But that biker ran a red light! If we'd collided, it would have been his fault.

Not that it matters. If I end up dead, I won't even be able to explain that to the police. And when the light cycles back to me, I look both ways very carefully before scurrying across the avenue like a frightened squirrel.

I've only been in New York for eight hours or so. But it isn't going that well. I'm tired. My feet are killing me.

Worst of all, I feel no closer to getting a job than I did when I boarded the flight in Burlington this morning.

My hotel room beckons. I'm staying at a low-budget chain, but this one is new enough that it gets decent reviews on Trip-Advisor. I push open the smudged glass door and roll my little suitcase across the hard floor toward the check-in desk. If they gave my room away, I just might break down and cry.

They didn't give it away. So that's something.

But after the bored-looking check-in guy hands me a key and sends me to the fourth floor, I discover the smallest hotel room I've ever seen. There is literally no room for anything besides the bed. It's like a prison cell, and the only window looks out onto a shaft-like space so narrow that I can only see other hotel curtains.

At least I can finally take off these shoes. I put them on the floor of the tiny closet. Then I remove my mother's old Sunday coat, and her blue jacket, hanging everything up in the closet. I take a shower and carefully dry my hair so it won't do anything crazy overnight.

But then there's nothing left to do. So I pull back the unfamiliar bedclothes and get into the bed with my phone. I set the alarm to wake me up on time tomorrow.

But I don't know how well I can sleep in this odd little gray box. There are voices in the hallway, bickering in another language. I should find it new and fascinating. But instead I just feel lost.

I *want* to love New York. I had this vision of moving to the big city and starting my life over from scratch. People do that all the time, right?

But I don't feel so fierce and brave right now. I feel untethered. As if this tiny Lego brick of a room could tumble off the tower and take me with it forever. In fact, if I disappeared tonight, nobody would even know where to look for me. Except my credit card company, nobody even knows that I came to this hotel.

My phone chimes with a text, and I feel an answering zap of relief. I need someone to talk to right now before I tip over the steep precipice of my unplanned life.

I grab the phone. The text is from the airline, reminding me to check in for my flight back to Burlington tomorrow.

Well, crap. I feel a wave of loneliness so powerful it threatens to sweep me under. So I tap Carly's name and shoot

her a quick message. *Your shoes are cute but they hate me now.
I can't wait to give them back*.

Then I realize Carly is at work right now, slinging wings
and beer without me. And I have a really unhealthy shimmy of
longing for the Biscuit, of all places.

Get a grip, Abbi. There's no need to get sentimental for my
crappy job. Besides, it's not like I'd see Weston tonight. Table
seventeen won't be there. They're on their way to Indiana.

This lonely, needy girl shouldn't text him, right? Weston is
not my emotional support animal. I'm a friend with benefits.
My role is to be a good time. A *fun* time.

But it's fun to wish someone a good game, right? Right.
Whee! Fun!

Yup, I'm losing my mind. But I text him anyway. *Hi
Westie! Have a great weekend. Make Notre Dame cry!* Then I
add a GIF of a West Highland terrier barking.

He answers me a minute later. *Thanks, Abbster! How'd it
go today?*

Okay. Maybe. We'll see. Then my thumbs just tap out
another text. I can't help myself. *Can I call you?*

*Give me an **hour***, he replies. *I'll call you.*

It's a very long hour. When I get up to turn on the hotel TV,
I discover that the thing doesn't work. When I hit the power
button, it lights up before immediately fading back to black.

I suppose I could complain. They might move me to a
different room. But that's a lot of hassle. The thing is bolted to
the wall, because there's no room for a piece of furniture to
support it.

Once when I was a little kid, our TV started flickering right
as Mom and I set ourselves up to watch a movie together. "Oh
no, Mama!" I'd panicked, thinking movie night was off.

"*Hell* no," my mom had said, getting up off the couch,

crossing to that TV and delivering a sharp smack to its hulking rear.

And I swear the picture snapped right into view. Like it was terrified to disobey her. Then we'd cheered like crazy people.

I miss her so much. It doesn't help to think about that right now, though, when I'm already throwing myself a pity party in a soulless hotel between job interviews. I can't succumb to that kind of magical thinking. *If I could hug her just* one *more* *time*...

My phone lights up with an incoming video chat from Weston, and I grab it like the lifeline that it is. I accept the call, and his handsome face comes into view. He's grinning at me. "Abbi! What's shakin'?"

"Nothing much." I drink in his smile and his eyes that crinkle in the corners when he's joking around. And the tightness inside my chest begins to lift. "What's it like flying with the hockey team?"

"Noisy," he says. "And when somebody says something asinine, you're embarrassed because he's wearing the same damn jacket you are."

"That's irritating," I agree. "All the asinine things people blamed me for today were things I said myself."

He winces. "Interviews went that well, huh?"

"It's just hard to stand out in a crowd. Apparently the investment bank takes a tenth of the people who apply. I thought if they were flying me here, that meant I had a chance."

"You do have a chance," he points out.

"I guess." But I realize now that I was unprepared. I thought terrific grades and a willingness to work hard were all that I needed to show. But I'd overheard some interviewees throwing around opinions about the GDP and the yield curve and equity derivatives. I know what all those things are, but I don't have opinions about them.

I just didn't understand how it all worked. And now I am blue.

"How about that other bank?" he asks.

"Oh, it was… interesting." I picture the round-faced man who'd sat across from me at that other interview. "The guy kept staring at my chest, and it threw me off."

Weston groans. "I'm sorry."

"It's fine," I mumble. Because I hadn't done that well otherwise. The man had asked me why I wanted to work in mortgage origination. You'd think I would have seen that one coming. But I'd gone blank for a second, as his eyes took another trip to the open button on my blouse.

The truth is that I don't have strong feelings about mortgage origination, either. *Everyone needs a home to live in,* I'd said eventually. *It seems like a compassionate kind of banking.*

"Let's just say I'm hoping that tomorrow's interviews go better. But enough about me." I squint at the screen. Behind a shirtless Weston is a white tile wall. His tattoos stand out in the bright light. "Where are you right now? It almost looks like you're in—"

"The bathtub!" he says gleefully. "I'm giving my roommate some privacy."

"Why?" I blurb. "Wait, never mind. Maybe I don't need to know."

He chuckles. "He's just talking to his girl on the phone. Or at least that's all they were doing when I left. Now that I think about it, I should probably be afraid to leave this bathtub."

"I thought you guys would be partying in the lobby."

"No way," he says. "Coach is very firm with his curfew on game night. Once a year somebody sneaks out and does something stupid. And then they usually get caught. It ain't pretty. But some people have to learn lessons the hard way."

I smile at the tiny screen, and feel lighter. Weston is like sunshine on a cloudy day. "Tell me one dumb thing that somebody did."

"Well, one time—during spring playoffs—there was a Dutch women's field hockey team staying in the same hotel…"

I start smiling again before he's even finished the sentence.

TWENTY-ONE

IS THAT A EUPHEMISM?

Weston

I tell Abbi a funny story involving a four-way room rearrangement that once became necessary just to give two couples some privacy. "There were more bed swaps that night than in a British sexual farce."

Abbi giggles. She's lying on a bed, wearing flannel PJs with little bunnies all over them. And I just wish I were there.

"Speaking of hotel beds..." I say, sounding about as subtle as a freight train. "This is a travesty. We're both in hotels. If it were the *same* hotel, we could be having hotel sex right now."

"That would definitely improve my day," she admits, propping her cheek in her hand. "If anyone is going to stare at my chest, I choose you."

"*See?* That's why all the lust-filled thoughts I have about you are okay. I'm on the VIP list. You just *invited* me to stare at your tits."

"It's a very short VIP list," she says with a smile. "With just one name on it."

"Yeah, I like it that way." Even as the words leave my

mouth, I realize how true they are. Abbi and I are supposed to be just a casual thing. But I feel a little possessive of her, which really isn't fair. I have nothing to give her for the long term.

And yet, if she met someone new tomorrow—some guy at her new job, who wanted to go the distance—I wouldn't like it one bit. This school year still has three months left, and I plan to take advantage of every one of them.

"What are you thinking about so hard?" Abbi asks suddenly. And I realize I've been lost in thought for no good reason.

"Your tits, of course." It's not strictly true. But seeing as I think about them with some frequency, it might as well be.

Abbi unbuttons just one button on her PJs, and suddenly I can see the soft swells of her cleavage. "There. Now you and the mortgage banker have the same view."

My body tightens deliciously. The bathwater has me feeling warm and loose already. "You're killing me right now. When am I going to see you next—for real?"

"Hard to say," she says. "I work a double on Sunday."

"When do you get off?" I ask. By which I mean, *when can I get you off?* Making Abbi whimper and sigh is my new favorite hobby.

"Eight," she says. "A double shift on Sunday means you don't have to close."

"Come over? We'll be hanging out at the hockey house, drinking some beers and unwinding."

"Maybe I can," she says. "What's the vibe at the hockey house, anyway? What's it like?"

"Not as skeevy as you're probably thinking," I say and she laughs. "I mean—we have some killer parties. But on a quieter night it's comfortable. Our alumni landlords make sure the place has a weekly cleaning service and every TV channel under the sun. The kitchen is actually pretty sweet. We've got a giant blender that we use all the time, and a big mixer that we never use, but it looks *very* sophisticated."

Abbi laughs again. "The things I could do with that mixer."

"My mixer is your mixer, baby. What do you want to mix?"

"I found a recipe in my mother's cookbook for this weird cake she used to make for me. I haven't had it in years..." Her smile fades, and she looks a little wistful.

"Seriously, if you want to putter in my kitchen, you can do that anytime. But come over Sunday either way, okay?" *Because I miss you.* I don't say that part out loud. "We'll be watching tonight's Bruins game," I say instead. "We made a pact on the plane to save it until after we get back."

She blinks. "So I shouldn't tell you they're losing four to zip?"

"Wait, really?" I gasp. "*Four* to nothing?"

Her smile blooms naughtily. "You're so *gullible*, Westie. I really have no idea if the Bruins are playing tonight or not."

"Abbi!" I laugh, and try not to drop my phone in the tub. "You're so mean. Maybe you should show me some more tit as a punishment. Two minutes for unsportsmanlike conduct."

"You want penalty tits?" she asks with a giggle.

"Oh, definitely."

She reaches up... and buttons the PJs closed instead.

I let out a little moan of frustration.

"Let's wait," she says. "Until you can see them in real life. I'm not comfortable flashing you over hotel Wi-Fi."

"Ah, fine. Fine." I suppose she's being smart about that, even if I'm crushed. "Just so you know, I'm not as smart as you are. And I'm not shy. So..." I lift the phone and change the angle. First I reveal my abs, which I'm tightening for the occasion. The six-pack is looking pretty buff onscreen, if I do say so myself.

Abbi makes a small sound of pleasure.

So I keep going. I angle the phone even further, until she can see my erect cock poking mostly out of the bathwater. "Look who says hello."

"Well, *hi* there," she breathes, her lips parted. "Now I really *do* wish we were at the same hotel."

"Yeah, well." I reach down and give myself a slow stroke, and Abbi makes another noise of approval. "You like that? Or am I just being creepy right now?"

She smiles. "You're *not* creepy, Weston. Everything you do is sexy. Every. Thing."

A warmth hits me that has nothing to do with bathwater. "You know I think the same thing about you, right? Everything you do is sexy."

"No need to exaggerate."

"Oh, I'm not." I give myself another slow stroke, because it feels so good. "If you were here, you'd be in this tub with me. I'd insist."

"Mmm," she sighs. "If only."

My voice goes low and rough just thinking about it. "We'll put that on our bucket list. Things to do together before we run out of time together."

"I'm in," she whispers. "Keep, uh, going. If you want to."

"You want me to?" My voice is pure gravel. "Put on a show for you?"

"Yes. Does that make me a hypocrite?"

"No," I insist. "We all have our comfort levels. Mine is set on *slutty*."

She laughs. On the screen, she seems to sink a little further back into the pillows. Then she licks her lips. "I admire that. Mine is stuck on *cautious*."

"You've had to be," I remind her. But my mind is only half present in this conversation. "Hang on. I need to make a few adjustments."

It's just your ordinary Thursday night right here at the Marriott, with me setting up to tug one out in the bathtub on a video call with my fuck buddy. Luckily, the hotel bathtub has a shelf that stretches across it—for your glass of wine, I guess—with a groove across it for your e-reader or whatever. I prop up my phone on the shelf, which frees up my hands.

Then I grab the little body wash bottle and squirt some into my palm. Now my hand is all slicked up, and I run it casually over my chest and my neck, while Abbi lets out a breathy gasp. "If I were there, I'd do that for you," she whispers.

I feel her gaze like a caress. Enough teasing. I drop my hand to my stiff cock and take myself in a firm, slick grip. I tease the underside with my thumb, and it feels so good I let out a horny groan.

"Whew," Abbi sighs. "It's suddenly really hot in here."

I don't respond, because I'm watching her flushed face on the screen as she licks her lips. She likes this. A lot. Then I see her slide a hand up under her top.

"Are you...oh *hell* yes." She's touching her breasts under her shirt. I see the form of her hand circling her nipple. And now her eyes are going dark and dreamy.

Damn this is fun. And I love pushing Abbi's boundaries just a little bit.

A few minutes ago I'd called myself slutty. Except I've never done this before. I haven't had a girlfriend since high school, and therefore nobody to get freaky on camera with.

I pump myself and realize two things at once. The first is that this isn't going to take very long. Abbi's heated gaze is burning me up.

The second is that this only *looks* slutty. It's actually just the opposite. You have to trust someone an awful lot to stroke your cock while she watches. You have to trust that she'll find it hot instead of ridiculous. And that she won't take screenshots and post them on the Internet.

Abbi would never do that. I know it with perfect confidence. Just like I also know that I haven't trusted anyone else like that in a *long* time. I haven't wanted to. I haven't seen the point.

But suddenly it's clear as day that I do trust her, as I tip my head back against the tile and work my slick hand up and down my shaft. Then I drop my free hand down to tug on my balls.

Abbi lets out a little moan when I do that. And I swear the sound is what starts to push me over the edge. "Fuuuuck, honey. Miss you." My hand pumps away. Release is calling my name.

"Miss *you*, Weston," she whispers. "Wish I could show you how much."

And that's what gets me off. My balls go tight and then sweet relief finally arrives. She gasps as I come on my chest. My jaw is locked tight as I milk it for all it's worth.

But then I sag against the porcelain. I feel strangely wrecked. Now I'm just a messy guy in a cooling tub, who wishes he could curl up in a bed with the bright-eyed sweetheart on the screen.

If I wasn't ridiculous before, I am now, right? This is why they never show you the aftermath in porn. I look red faced and crazy eyed. And I feel almost hung over.

So I reach up and turn off my camera. Then I lift the phone to my ear. "Well, I hope that was better than what's on TV," I say casually.

Abbi lets out a hungry moan in my ear. "That was..." She swallows. "Wow."

I smile through my unexpected embarrassment. "Sunday night, then?"

"You know it," she says with a little laugh.

"Eight o'clock," I whisper.

"Okay," she agrees. "I might bring the ingredients for a cake."

"Is that a euphemism?"

"No. But you like cake, right? I'm not sleeping with some kind of psycho?"

"You know I like cake." I open the drain on the bathtub. "But I don't know how much sleeping I'm going to let you do. Bring your toothbrush anyway."

"I will. Good night, Westie."

"Good night, Abbster. I'll dream about you." That's another thing I've never said before. I'm racking up all the firsts tonight.

We sign off, and I stand up and shower myself off. I feel a little skittish now, and it's hard to say why. It's just a little fun with Abbi. No big deal, right?

Right. No big deal.

I turn off the shower and grab a towel. Yup, just an ordinary Thursday night in South Bend. Nothing to see here.

TWENTY-TWO

WHERE THE MAGIC HAPPENS

Abbi

Working a double shift always seems long. But Sunday's seems to drag on forever. I'm excited to see Weston. *Really* excited. I tell myself that it's just the sex, which is epic.

But it's scary how much I really like him. And the fact that he seems to like me too is giving me all kinds of romantic ideas that I shouldn't be having. Whenever I catch myself daydreaming about him, I want to slap myself.

He hasn't offered me a future. But he did offer me his kitchen. So earlier today I bought the ingredients to make a huge vanilla cake with pecan praline icing, just like my mother used to make.

Meanwhile, I'm waiting tables on what has turned out to be a hellishly busy Sunday. Carly is in a surprisingly bad mood, too. But it's been too crazy for me to corner her and figure out why.

There's finally a lull at quarter to eight, and I catch up to her by the soda machine. "Hey," she says, a tired look on her face. "Any chance you want to close for me?"

"Oh, crap. I really can't. I, um..."

She laughs. "You have plans with a certain defenseman who won against Notre Dame last night?"

"I do," I whisper. "But keep quiet about that."

"Of course. And I'll stick it out here." Carly's expression droops.

"Are you okay?" I press. "If you really need me to stay, I will. You worked for me on Thursday."

"How did it go in New York, anyway?"

"It's hard to say." I tell her about my dodgy interviews on Thursday. "And then on Friday I interviewed for the marketing teams at two fun, girly brands."

"That sounds better."

"You'd think," I grumble. "But they just want social media coverage." And they were intimidating in a completely different way. At both interviews I was asked which were my favorite designers.

I'm way too poor to have favorite designers. So I'd had to twist the question around and explain which clothing brands were doing the most interesting things on social media. And that worked pretty well, I guess.

I don't think I stuck the landing at either company. And I came home feeling defeated. "But enough about me," I say. "What's got you down?"

She shakes her head. "I'm fine, Abbi."

"You don't seem fine," I argue. "Seriously. Will you tell me what's bothering you?"

She opens her mouth and then closes it and shakes her head. "I don't want to stress you out with my drama."

"But that's what friends do, right?"

Carly looks torn. And I'm mentally tearing up my evening plans to close for her if she needs me to. "I had a run-in with Price," she says.

165

My stomach drops. "Oh no. When?"

"Yesterday afternoon."

"But bouncers don't work afternoons. Where did you see him?"

"Here." She winces. "He's training to be a bartender. You know how they train people on the lunchtime shift?"

"You are *kidding* me!" I yelp. "This is terrible."

She nods grimly. We both know that Kippy is strapped for bartending help. One time Carly and I offered to train as bartenders, because the tips are better. But Kippy prefers men. And he had the balls to tell us right to our faces that he wouldn't let us try it because we're the best servers he has.

Neither of us wants to argue ahead of our bonus anniversaries, either.

"It gets worse," she hisses. "Price made a point to tell me that he'll be seeing a lot *more* of me. Then he grabbed my ass when I was standing at the touchscreen working on an order."

"I hate him," I whisper.

"Two more months," Carly whispers back. "That's all I have to stick this out until my bonus check. Let's not panic yet," she says, although she looks to be doing that very thing.

"Okay," I agree just as the bartender on shift dings his little bell. "That's my last drink order for the night. I've already dropped the check, too."

"Go," Carly says, shooing me. "Go be with your man. I'll be fine, Abbi. We both will."

I'm sure she's right. I've survived Price before. I can do it again.

The hockey house is a big, multipeaked Victorian home just off campus. The lights are blazing from inside as I climb the stairs to the big porch. My arms are weighed down by a shopping bag full of groceries, and I'm feeling a little foolish.

Lots of women go to parties at the hockey house. It's just that I've never been one of them. The total number of college parties I've attended is a pretty low number. I started college less than a year after my mother's death, when I still lived in Dalton's home. Both grief and a long commute prevented me from becoming a partier. That was a dark time, and I'm lucky I got decent grades and stayed in school.

So it almost feels like I'm visiting a foreign country as I approach the door.

Before I can reach for the doorbell, the door flies open, and Weston's smiling face appears. "Abbi! You made it! Let me take that." He opens the screen door and takes the bag with one of his strong arms.

And then? He uses the other one to scoop me into a kiss.

A really good kiss.

Top-notch.

When he pulls away, it's too soon. "Somebody's been hard up for a week," I whisper. And I might mean me.

Weston doesn't reply. His warm eyes crinkle at the corners as he smiles, and I get one more kiss on the temple. "Come in. I made the freshmen clean the kitchen, just in case you were serious about making a cake."

"Oh, I was dead serious."

"Awesome. Come on, let me show you the place." He turns to carry my grocery bag into the house.

I straighten my spine and follow him into the living room, where a dozen or so hockey players and various women are perched all over the furniture. The Bruins game is playing on a giant TV on the wall.

"This is where the magic happens," Weston says, indicating the whole first level of the house with a sweep of his arm. "If by magic you mean a lot of debauchery and smack talk."

"Noted." I peel off my coat and Weston hangs it on a coat rack. And I swear every head in the room swings around to stare at us.

"Uh, guys. You remember Abbi from the Biscuit."

"Hi, Abbi," several voices call out in unison.

"Tonight she's our guest, yeah?" Weston says. "That means her glass is never empty."

"Got it," says a freshman who's seated on the floor. I guess the furniture is for upperclassmen.

"Good," Weston says. Then he takes my hand and leads me into the kitchen.

He hadn't been joking. It's a great kitchen—not fancy, but spacious. There's a big table with eight chairs, too. And my favorite appliance—the mixer—gleams in the corner. "Wow. Time to cream some butter and sugar."

"Cream? Oh honey, *yessss!*" He lets out a salacious moan.

"You perv."

He grins. "How about I help you with this cake? Then I can perv out later."

"Don't you have a game you're supposed to be watching?"

Even as I say these words, a loud chorus of groans erupts in the living room. And one lonely cheer.

"You hear that?" Weston points over his shoulder with his thumb. "I think I can follow the game from here. The Bruins just got scored on."

"Someone was happy," I point out as I unpack butter, sugar, and flour from my bag.

"One of the freshmen is a Rangers fan." Weston makes a face.

"And you allow that?"

"We tolerate it. Nobody's perfect."

You are. Ugh. It's inconvenient how much I like Weston. I know we're just a temporary thing. But I am going to miss him fiercely when I move away. "Will you preheat the oven to 350?"

"Sure." But he doesn't do it. Instead, he moves to stand behind me. Then he lifts my hair and kisses my neck.

My body flashes hot, and goose bumps rise up on my arms. He kisses me again, his lips soft and yet insistent. "Westie, don't take this as a criticism. But it's hard to make cake when you're so distracting."

"I know." He sighs. "Okay. Put me to work. Keep my hands busy, or I'm going to have to find other uses for them."

"Right. First the oven, and then..." I pull a printed copy of my mother's recipe out of my coat pocket. "Can you measure out three cups of pecans? We have to chop them and then fry them in butter."

"You got it," he says.

The living room lets out a sudden cheer.

"Ooh, score!" Weston says, pulling open the bag of pecans. "Let's do this."

TWENTY-THREE

THIS MIGHT TAKE A WHILE

Weston

I've lived in this house for a year and a half, but I've never baked a cake in this kitchen. That seems like a mistake now, because the house smells *amazing*. And it's surprisingly fun assisting Abbi with her mixing and scraping.

Once the cake is in the oven, and the timer is set, I have an easier time stealing kisses. I push Abbi up against the counter and take her mouth with the same furor that I usually save for stealing the puck.

Abbi melts against my body. Her mouth softens under mine, and her arms wrap around my neck.

I'm just wondering whether there's enough time to drag her upstairs for a quickie before the oven timer dings, when she pushes me away with gentle hands. "Westie, I have to make the frosting. Caramelization takes some time. Do you have a skillet?"

"Yes, ma'am," I say, because it's more polite than ripping her clothes off. Then I find the woman a skillet.

Abbi melts another stick of butter in the pan and then

tosses the pecans in. She stirs them continuously and takes frequent sniffs of the pan.

"What is that for?" I ask.

"My mom's instructions say to cook it until it smells 'caramelly,' and then start adding the powdered sugar. This might take a while."

"Want a drink? There are beers in the fridge."

"Sure," she says brightly. "Thanks."

I get us each a beer. And then the living room erupts in shouting and confusion.

Hmm.

"You'd better go see what just happened," Abbi says. She gives me a little push on the hip. "Sounds like a bad call from the ref."

"Right back," I tell her.

"Take your time. I got this."

As I head for the living room, I glance back at Abbi. She's humming to herself and stirring the pecans. She looks happy.

I feel pretty damn happy, too. I've got hockey and beer and the sweet scent of cake. And—even better—I've got more of Abbi's kisses coming at me later. I can't wait to drag her up to my lair and show her how much I've missed her.

"What do you look so happy about?" Tate asks on a growl when I arrive at his side. "The ref just gave this game away."

"Look on the bright side," I point out. "At least he didn't just give *our* game away."

"I guess," he grumbles. "There's still ten minutes in the period. We can rebuild it."

Due to an unfortunate glance at my news feed this morning, I already know that we didn't, in fact, rebuild it. But I'll keep my trap shut, and I cock my hip against the doorway and watch Boston fight for it anyway.

I'm cheering on the goalkeeper when the front door opens and a familiar face appears.

"Hey guys!" It's Amy, a teammate's little sister. She goes to Champlain College—which is the other college in Burlington. And every so often she swings by with a friend or two. In fact, last time that happened I hooked up with—

Uh-oh. After Amy clears the door, another face appears. Her friend is cute and bubbly. I remember we had a good time together. But it was only the one time, of course. But now her gaze locks onto mine, and there's a fire in her eye that spells trouble.

And here I'd thought that a non-Moo-U student was a winning hookup choice. I'd assumed the odds of us coming face-to-face again were pretty low. Not low enough, as it turns out. She tosses her coat onto a hook and makes a beeline for me.

Oh shit.

Even though I'm always up-front with my hookups, this happens once in a while. I make my little speech the same way every time, before any clothes come off. *So, listen, I'm not in a position to start anything serious. But if you're up for one night of fun, I'm your guy.*

Not everyone's hearing is great, I suppose.

"Weston, hey! It's been a while," she says. She holds out her arms, as if expecting me to kiss her hello.

I don't, though. Instead, I stand up a little straighter and give her a smile that's friendly but not encouraging. "How've you been…" It takes me a second to pull her name from my memory. "Kerry?"

"Cara," she says quickly.

Shit. *"Cara,* God. Sorry. Well it's been a while."

"Yeah. No kidding."

I see my buddy Tate start to smile at me from a couple

yards away. He can sense my distress. But does he come over here and rescue me?

Nope. No such luck.

Cara moves closer. She puts a hand on my chest. "Anyway, I thought I'd hitch a ride with Savannah and see if you were up for hanging out tonight."

Tate hides his mocking grin behind his beer, and I want to slug my teammate. Because, Christ, this is a train wreck. "Uh, Cara, the thing is..." And then I come screeching to a halt, because this isn't a speech I've made before. *There's someone else.* That sounds like a line from a drama.

I'm still choosing my words when Abbi materializes at my side. "Cake's out of the oven!" she says brightly.

"Oh, awesome!" I slide an arm around her automatically—the same way I've done a half dozen times already tonight.

But Cara goes rigid. And her face turns red so fast that someone should probably call the fire department.

"Could you help me invert it?" Abbi asks. "I need a largish plate if you've got one."

"Plate. Large. Yup," I say, stumbling badly. "I've got that. Baby."

Abbi gives me a sideways glance that seems to wonder if I've sustained a hit to the head. "Okay. It needs to cool for five more minutes, but then it's go time." She kisses the underside of my jaw before peeling away, heading back to the kitchen.

Meanwhile, Cara keeps turning redder. "Looks like you're a little busy," she says quickly. "Take care." Then, before I can say anything, she slips past me and heads up the stairs in the direction that Amy disappeared.

Several of my teammates watch her ascent. And when she's good and gone, they turn to me.

"Awkward," says Vonne. "I sense a story there."

"It's a short story," Paxton chirps from the sofa. "They always are with Weston."

"That's not true," Vonne points out. "Weston has a girlfriend."

"You're a freshman," Tate says. "You haven't seen how it goes with him. We're all a little surprised that he and Abbi have been together these past couple of weeks."

"Right?" another of my teammates puts in. "Weston doesn't date. It's an unwritten rule of hockey."

"You mean, like, the fight ends when your opponent goes down?" Vonne asks with a smirk. "And never step on the logo in the middle of the locker room floor?"

"Like that," Tate assures him. "But Abbi is breaking all the rules."

I give him a withering glance that suggests he should keep his voice down. "Abbi is the exception that proves the rule."

Vonne raises his hand, like a second-grader. "What does that even mean? That phrase makes no sense."

"Sure it does," I bark, even though this whole conversation makes me uncomfortable.

"What it *means*," Tate whispers, "Is that Abbi graduates in the spring. Weston here doesn't have to worry about a real commitment."

"Ooh, an older woman," Vonne says. "Love it."

I roll my eyes at both of them. Tate isn't wrong. It's just that I'm not enjoying listening to my love life being picked apart.

So I leave them behind and head into the kitchen to help Abbi find a plate for her cake. The air here is heavy with the scent of nuts and sugar. "Holy shitballs, that smells good."

"Doesn't it?" Abbi says. "This was the cake my mother made for my birthday every year. It's a straightforward cake recipe, but with this crazy pecan icing. You can only eat a small slice before you start to slide into diabetic shock. So a whole cake would last us a week in the refrigerator."

"I give it a half hour in this joint," I tell her. "So cut yourself a nice slice. You have to look after your own needs at the hockey house."

"I'm starting to understand that," she mutters to herself.

TWENTY-FOUR

A LOT OF BROKEN HEARTS

Abbi

I'm on my back in Weston's bed. He's hovering over me in the plank position, languorously thrusting, while I pant against his tongue and try not to moan too loudly.

"Fuck, Abbi," he curses. "I don't want it to end. You get me so hot."

He says this as if I might not understand. As if I'm not the one who's splayed naked on his bed, legs wide apart, worshiping at the altar of Weston's dirty talk and growly kisses.

Is this real life?

"Touch yourself, baby."

"W-what?" I whisper.

"Touch yourself and let me watch." He looks down at me, eyes gleaming. "I did it on camera. You can do it in bed, right? There's nobody to see but me. And I *really* want to see."

He punctuates this big idea with another steamy, brain-bending kiss. And I can't think anymore. I can't remember who

I was before I became Weston's plaything. And I can't remember why I should ever leave his bed. Everything is perfect here.

"Go on," he rasps. "I want to watch."

So I don't even hesitate. I reach down between our bodies and slowly stroke myself, while Weston presses himself up on his delectable arms and drinks in the sight of us merging together.

"*Fuuuck*," he breathes. "Get there for me, Abbi. I need to hear you come."

And I do—instantly—and it's probably because my fragile little heart heard those first three words the loudest: "*I need you.*"

If only he truly meant it.

Afterward, we lie together in a blissed-out, sweaty heap. This must be what heaven is like. We've had cake. We've had fantastic sex. And even now, Weston is stroking my back, staring into my eyes, looking at me like I matter.

I want to believe him. So badly. But the problem is that I know better. Tonight has been great. But it's also offered me a painful reminder of how things really are.

Weston's kitchen provides near perfect acoustics into the living room. So I'd heard that girl arrive—Cara. And I'd happened to peek out of the kitchen, watching and listening while he blundered her name.

He'd felt bad about it. Weston isn't an asshole.

But maybe I am. Because something propelled me to step out and claim him. I could blame hormones, I guess. The truth is that I feel a giddiness at being Weston's woman of the hour. And when he'd slipped an arm around my shoulder, I felt like a queen.

But then? When I'd gone back into the kitchen, I'd also

overheard Tate and Vonne ribbing Weston about his allergy to commitment. That had been hard to hear, even if I knew it was the truth.

Weston and I will be separated the minute after I graduate. He'll become my nicest memory of my time at Moo U. But I already know that he won't become my long-term boyfriend—either fake or otherwise.

Still, when I'm able to live in the moment, life is pretty great. After Weston and I had inverted the cake onto a big platter he'd found in a cupboard, I'd iced it with my gooey pecan frosting. Then I let it cool a little so the icing could set.

Weston had suggested we watch the end of the game before treating a house full of hockey players to cake. And I'd sat tucked against him in the living room. Together we'd watched the last half hour of the game. And every fifteen minutes, a freshman refilled my soda glass, just as Weston had ordered.

That'd meant I needed to pee. So when the game was nearly over, I'd climbed the stairs to the second floor to use Weston's bathroom.

As I walked along the carpet runner stretching down the hallway, I'd heard voices spilling out from behind a door that was open a crack.

"I'm such an idiot," the girl had sobbed. "I really thought he liked me."

It was Cara. And I'd frozen in place, shamelessly eavesdropping.

"Even though he never answered your texts?" her friend had prompted gently.

"I thought maybe he changed numbers."

"Oh, Cara."

"I know, okay? I *know*. It's just hard to understand. We had a *great* time that night. Not just a hot time. I felt a real connection. We talked half the night. And the sex was over the top."

"Oh honey. I'm sorry. Weston is…"

I'd stopped breathing.

"He leaves a lot of broken hearts in his wake. It's not intentional, I bet. He just has this talent for making everyone feel special. But connection isn't his end goal. It's fun."

"I *am* fun," her friend had sobbed.

"Right, but you live across town, so he's already forgotten how much fun you are. He avoids entanglements, Cara. He lives in the moment."

"Ugh," she'd said, and I'd heard copious nose-blowing. "It just stings. I've been thinking about him since November. But he didn't spend any of that time thinking about me."

Then she'd dissolved into tears again, and I'd hurried toward the bathroom.

That poor girl. My heart breaks for her, because I'm pretty sure her friend has it exactly right. Weston is just like she said —a great guy who lives for fun, with a talent for making everyone feel special.

Right this moment he's massaging my shoulder with a loving hand. I feel the same wonderful connection between us that Cara had. But one day soon I'll *be* Cara. I'll be sitting in my tiny New York apartment, wishing he'd return my texts.

Or maybe I'll run into Weston someday at a reunion. He'll call me Amy or Annie. "*It's Abbi*," I'll say.

And he'll feel bad that he's forgotten. But he *will* have forgotten.

Just ask Cara.

"Abbi," he says suddenly. And I startle, as if my thoughts are so loud that he might overhear them.

"Mmm?" I say casually. As if any of this were casual for me. Maybe Weston doesn't know how to do commitment, but I'm

179

just the opposite. I crave commitment. And love. A family, and a place to call home. All the things I don't have in my life.

"Where did you go?" he asks.

"No place at all," I assure him, lifting my face to smile at him. "I'm right here."

It's just that I wish I could stay. Even though I know I can't.

TWENTY-FIVE

PROPERTY OF ABBI AND WESTON

Weston

I wake up in an empty bed. Rolling over, I look around for Abbi. But she's not here.

Her phone is, though. In fact, I think her ringing phone is what just woke me up. When I grab it off the bedside table, the screen says: *Caller is DALTON.*

Even though the call has already gone to voicemail, I decide that it could be important. So I heave my groggy self into an upright position and don the Westie pants Abbi gave me for Christmas. Then I start looking for her.

It's just after seven a.m., so the house is quiet. Abbi is the only one awake. She's seated herself at the kitchen table, where the last two remaining slices of cake are positioned with a card I'd printed before going to bed last night: PROPERTY OF ABBI AND WESTON. DO NOT EAT UNDER PENALTY Of DEATH.

"Cake for breakfast, huh?"

She startles. "I didn't hear you come downstairs." And when she meets my gaze, her eyes are red-rimmed.

"Hey, are you okay?"

"Of course."

Hmm. "Your eyes are red."

"That happens sometimes. I made coffee. I hope that's okay."

"Of course it's okay." I put her phone on the table. "This says that Dalton called."

"Oh! Sorry. Hope it wasn't too loud."

"It's fine, baby." She seems a little brittle, but I can't quite put my finger on why.

"I'll check to see if the coffee is done. Here's a fork." She positions the cake plate between us.

"Thank you."

Then she takes the phone and heads to the other end of the big kitchen, tapping the phone to make a call as she goes. "Hi Dalton," she says in a hushed voice. "Sorry I missed your call."

Her polite tone tears at me in a way that's hard to explain. Dalton is the only family she has left, but she speaks to him like he's the school principal. *I'm sorry I missed your call.* It's not even eight o'clock, for chrissakes.

"Noon. Sure. Thank you. I'll be ready. What's that?" Her eyes cut to mine. "I'm ninety percent sure he has class. But I'll double check. Of course." She reaches for two coffee mugs in the drying rack. "Thank you. Lunch is fine, really. I have to work at dinnertime. See you soon."

She hangs up the call and pours two cups of coffee. I'm watching her, trying to decide if I should ask her what that's all about, when I realize I'm letting her serve me a drink in my own damn home.

I leap up and grab the milk out of the fridge. "Thank you for the coffee. Now come and sit with me."

Abbi returns to the table and takes a fortifying gulp of coffee. But she still doesn't quite look like her normal, chipper self.

"Big plans with Dalton today?"

"I'm meeting him at noon," she says in a flat voice.

"Special occasion?" I press.

She sighs. "It's the third anniversary of my mother's death. We go to the cemetery every year."

My heart drops. "Oh Abbi, I'm sorry."

"Yeah, uh, thanks. It's just a shitty day. We get through it."

"Should I come along?" I hear myself ask. Because I'm pretty sure I heard Dalton make that invitation.

"No," she says quickly. "It's not fun."

"Well of *course* it isn't," I agree. "But neither was watching my family implode over Christmas."

Her eyes search me without really seeing me. "Dalton is taking me to lunch after. But you must have class today," she points out. "And then practice."

"Well, yeah," I admit. "And I have to get fitted for a tuxedo before my sister murders me."

She flashes me a quick smile. "Weston, you're busy. It's okay. Really." Then she ducks behind her coffee cup.

I feel uneasy. This is, to be fair, the kind of quandary that ride-or-die single guys avoid. I honestly don't know whether I'm supposed to insist on being there for Abbi, or not. "What about Price?" I ask. "Will you have to duck him today?"

Abbi shakes her head vigorously. "Price wouldn't dream of showing up to a cemetery. You don't have to do the fake boyfriend thing today."

Well, ouch. Because I guess I'm not showing up to one either. I really do have class, and it's a review session for a test I'm taking in two days.

"Okay," I say quietly. I pick up the fork and take a bite of cake. "This is really good stuff."

Abbi's smile is a flash, and then it's gone. "Thanks."

"It's awesome that you have her recipe."

"Yeah." Abbi picks up her fork and looks at the cake. But then she puts the fork down again. "I'm not, uh, hungry. You can finish this. Actually, I've got to run."

"But..."

Before I even manage to finish that sentence, she's on her way out of the kitchen.

Five minutes later she reappears with her backpack. She gives me a kiss on the cheek and reaches for her coffee mug. "I'll wash this before I head out."

I clamp down on her hand. "Leave it, Abbi. I can wash the damn mug."

"Okay," she says quickly, her eyes flashing with an emotion I can't quite read. "Later."

And then she's gone, and I'm sitting here feeling unsettled.

"Someone's an early riser," mutters Tate as he shuffles into the kitchen. "Your girl get you up early for sexy times?"

"No." I let out a sigh. "I might have screwed up with her."

"Might have?"

"Yeah. I'm not sure."

"Hmm." Tate points at the cake. "You eating all that?"

I pass him Abbi's clean fork. "We can go halfsies. She ran out of here without eating it."

"Hmm." He takes a bite. "You two have a fight?"

I shake my head. "I just don't know where the boundary lines are, you know? Abbi doesn't have an easy life."

"Do any of us?" Tate asks.

I know for a fact that Tate's family farm is struggling, and he somehow does chores there, works an extra job, and still makes it to hockey practice.

So the man has a point. "I guess everybody has their moments. But this is a bad moment for Abbi, and I don't know what I'm supposed to do."

"I thought it was casual with you two."

"It is," I insist.

"Then what are you worried about?"

"I'm not sure," I lie, and then I shove another bite of cake into my mouth. "Honestly, I'm starting to feel like Abbi deserves better than me. I'm a commitmentphobe with a busy schedule. She needs a guy who wants to go the distance. A real partner."

"She seems like a great girl," Tate says. "But she's graduating, right?"

"Right." I feel relief just saying it. "I won't let Abbi down, and she won't let me down. We'll just go our separate ways."

Tate's eyebrows lift. "Hang on, though. Did Abbi *say* she wants more from you?"

"Well…" I try to think. "No, she never said so. It's just a feeling I have." Don't most women want more of me?

Christ, maybe I'm just an egomaniac.

"See, you don't actually know." My friend shrugs. "She might not even be looking for a long-term thing. Maybe she's just as relieved as you are that it's off the table."

"Hmm." I sit with this idea for a moment. But it doesn't quite feel right. "Abbi keeps her cards pretty close to her chest. But I get the feeling she can't let herself expect more from anyone in her life. She's really alone in the world."

"Like how alone?"

"An orphan. She has a stepdad, but he remarried. And there's a new step-stepbrother who sexually harasses her."

"Wait—that bouncer at the Biscuit?" Tate asks.

"That's the guy."

Tate makes a face like he's tasted something foul. "That guy is a tool."

"Yeah, and he's the reason she can't even live in her stepfather's home. She's got a lot on her plate. And life has already disappointed her so brutally…"

"You don't want to be the next thing that goes wrong for her," Tate suggests.

"Exactly."

He shakes his head. "That's tricky. Because you got your issues, but Abbi's got more. She's not a starter girlfriend."

"A *what?*"

"She needs a pro, right? Not someone who gets itchy about commitment."

"Right," I agree.

"Hmm," Tate says. "Did you end up inviting her to your sister's wedding in May?"

"No, I didn't," I say slowly. "I doubt Abbi will still be around by then."

"Maybe that's for the best," Tate says. "It sends a whole other message, you know? Weddings make people crazy."

"Yeah? I'm pretty sure marriage makes people crazy. But weddings just make people drunk and horny."

"I dunno, man." Tate grins. "Be careful who you take to a wedding. All that devotion and commitment is, like, contagious. Not that there's anything wrong with that. But you gotta be ready to receive that pass when the winger sends it."

"Yeah. Thanks for the advice." I drain my coffee. Devotion and commitment are not a good look on me. Sad but true.

Does that make me an asshole for spending time with Abbi?

I only wish I knew.

TWENTY-SIX
NOT THINKING BIG ENOUGH

Abbi

Dalton picks me up in a car that smells like roses. On the back seat waits a beautiful bouquet of multicolored flowers in a sturdy basket. I stare out the window at the overcast sky as he drives to the cemetery.

These past three years I've learned that grief is like a chronic disease. Some days are good days, and you barely think about it at all. But then there are the flare-ups, when you feel terrible and can't imagine ever feeling happy again.

Today it hurts. A lot. And I can't think of any reason why the pain should stop.

We arrive at her gravesite before I'm ready. Because I'll never be ready. And we climb out of Dalton's car into an empty parking lot.

Last year the snow was knee deep. But today there's only patchy snow and ice on the ground as we pick our way through the soggy, winter-brown grass.

This is a quiet little cemetery halfway between Burlington and Shelburne. But as I approach her headstone, I feel so much emptiness. My mother isn't really here. She's gone from this world. And this plot of brown, snow-clotted earth—with a generous hunk of granite carved with her name—is just a place that we go to have somewhere to put our sadness.

We need this place, though. Especially today. I take the roses out of Dalton's hands and place them carefully in front of the stone. They're beautiful, but I don't believe that she can actually see them.

Only Dalton and I can, as we shiver here under the winter sky, trying and failing to think of the right things to say to each other. I watch Dalton swipe a tear away, and I have to bear down to avoid my own from springing forth. If I cry right now, I might never stop.

It's excruciating. And yet I still see the point of this exercise. We either come here to purge ourselves of a small amount of our pain, or else we'll drown in it alone. I don't like it. But I understand it.

Next year, though, I probably won't be here. I'll be in an office somewhere in a distant city. Dalton will call me and tell me he delivered the roses. And I'll thank him.

Dalton is a good man. He loved my mother. He saw the joy inside her. He used to take her dancing. He even tried to teach her to play golf, but she couldn't seem to get the hang of it. So he switched her country club membership to "pool only" with a cheerful shrug.

I'm glad she had his love in her life, even if she was robbed of the years she deserved to enjoy it.

Mom, I guess you quit while you were ahead, I say inside my mind. *But I'm taking a serious deduction from your score for that terrible dismount.*

"Shall we?" Dalton says eventually, saving me from my awkward internal monologue.

"Yup."

We traipse back to the luxury car with its leather seats and the radio tuned to Vermont Public Radio.

But the scent of roses lingers all the way back to town.

Dalton takes me to The Farmhouse on Bank Street for lunch, where I discover that I'm famished. I order the burger with bacon and an excruciatingly locavore salad, and eat everything on my plate.

My lunch companion has a crab cake and a craft beer. We are shoring ourselves up, I suppose. But after the plates are cleared away, our conversation is still flagging. I feel as hollow as the environmentally correct paper straw that I keep worrying with my fingers.

Then Dalton breaks the silence with small talk about Vermont Tartan. "Taft said he hired you for some extra part-time hours after your internship ended."

"He did," I agree. "I was happy to do it, and his recommendation will help me get a job. Hopefully."

"He'll give you a glowing recommendation. But I don't understand why you two aren't going to work together after graduation."

I feel too weary to explain all the ways that social media jobs can be a trap. I'd be stuck taking pictures of Taft's dogs forever. "But it's such a small business," I point out. "It's Taft and Connie's baby. There's no room for me to do more than the social media stuff that they hate."

"Well, I told Taft that he's not thinking big enough," Dalton says. "Maybe they need someone like you to help them strategize for capturing a younger demographic."

"That's nice of you to say. But their daughter is coming aboard this summer, so they already have some new help."

"Alexis?" Dalton looks surprised. "I hadn't realized she was moving back to Vermont."

"True story." I've already met Alexis. She has two really cute toddlers and a perky outlook that is probably just what the business needs.

"Okay. Any other good job prospects?" Dalton asks.

"Let's not make this day any more depressing than it already is."

He shakes his head and gives me a smile. "All right. But if you need me to shake the trees at the country club, just say the word. Somebody will have something. Even if it's just temporary."

"I will absolutely keep that in mind," I say. Although it would feel like a huge step backward if I end up doing the bookkeeping for one of Dalton's doctor friends and picking up extra shifts at the Biscuit. I want a fresh start so badly.

"Some company is going to be very lucky to have you, Abbi. Just hang in there. And if you need to move back home after graduation, you know you could have your old room back."

My eyes fly to his in surprise. I don't even know what to say right now. Moving in with him is *not* an option. But it's nice of him to think it is.

"Your mother isn't here to look after you," he says gently. "The least I can do for her is to make sure you're okay."

"Thank you," I squeak. There's a new lump in my throat now.

"I know you'd prefer to be independent. Lord knows Price doesn't mind leaning on me a little. There's no reason you shouldn't do the same."

I swallow hard. And I'm *this* close to telling him why I can't live in a house where Price lives.

But then I remember what that would mean—driving a

wedge between Dalton and his new wife. I know Dalton pretty well by now. If I were forceful, he'd listen. But then I'd have to follow through. Dalton would probably make us all sit down as a "family" and talk to Price about boundaries.

Some people never learn boundaries, though. Price is one of those people.

The best thing to do is to stay the course. There has to be a good job out there somewhere for me. There are still three months until graduation. I'll find one.

I'll have to.

The very next day I get a rejection letter for the competitive training program in New York. Then I get a rejection from one of the social media jobs too.

And since I'm already a little depressed, I sink further into sadness.

This happens every winter. It's hard to keep my head above water during this time of year, with my mother's death looming so large in my mind. I'll never be able to look at the half-melted snowbanks without thinking about the day Dalton called me, voice shaking. *There's been an accident.*

I'm not very good company. But since the playoffs are coming, Weston is super busy. We're exchanging frequent texts and we speak occasionally on the phone. But we don't manage to spend time together before Weston heads out on another road trip to play Boston College.

I could really use a little distraction. Even my shifts at the Biscuit feel extra long.

"You look tired. Are you okay?" Carly keeps asking me.

"Sure," I respond. Because I will be eventually. At least I hope I will.

"We're overdue for a girls' night out," she insists. "Get out your phone. When's the next time neither of us is on shift here?"

The answer to that question does not improve my mood. We discover that our next opportunity to see each other outside work is three weeks out. "Better late than never, right?" she says. And we make a plan that's practically a life-time away.

The following week, table seventeen comes in for dinner right after practice. Weston gives me a big, happy smile. Even though Carly has their section tonight, I feel my mood lift just from seeing his face.

An hour later, hockey players start trickling out the door again. And Weston waves me over. "Hey, girly. Should I study at the bar and then walk you home?"

I check the time, and realize I don't get off work for another two hours. "Didn't you tell me you have a paper due tomorrow?"

"Yeah." He makes a face. "Sad but true."

"Go home," I decide. "Write in peace. I'll catch up with you this weekend."

"About that," he says. "My family is driving up Saturday for the Merrimack game. We're eating out first. Want to come?"

"Sure," I say immediately. "I haven't been to a game all season."

"Better late than never! I'll text you the details." He looks over both shoulders, scanning the room. And then he leans in and kisses me quickly. "Oops, I slipped. But Kippy isn't here. Bye, baby."

"Bye, Westie," I say in a dreamy voice I haven't used in a week.

Pleased with himself, he strides out.

Sending him off to study was the right thing to do. I'm awfully tired. Even if he came home with me, I might not be any fun. My feet ache from waiting tables. And my heart aches, too. I don't feel the least bit fun or sexy tonight. And I'd hate to let Weston down.

Forty minutes later, I'm waiting at the end of the bar when a hand slides across my ass.

I jump about a foot in the air and spin around to find Price grinning evilly at me. "Hey, Abbi. Where's your boyfriend now?"

"Fuck you," I spit. "What does it matter where he is? I'm not yours to touch. And it doesn't matter what you ever do, or ever say, I will *never* be yours to touch."

I hadn't meant to react. Ignoring him is my usual strategy. And now Price has murder in his eyes. Suddenly I'm in a terrifying staring contest with my least favorite man in Burlington.

Until Kippy barks my name. "*Abbi*. Table eight needs their check."

I whirl around and head for table eight, my heart in my mouth.

From now on I'd better watch my back.

I sleep terribly that night, and wake up Friday feeling light-headed and tired. But I head off to Vermont Tartan to help them sort out their social media accounts again.

But when I get there, the new intern doesn't show up. "Where's Margie?" I ask Taft after saying hello.

"She called in sick," he says. "There's some flu going around."

I fight off a shiver. Margie and I sat elbow to elbow the

other day, working on VT's Instagram account. "So you want me to just dive in?"

"If you wouldn't mind," he says. "Alexis left you some photographs of the spring line in your cloud folder. She loved what you and Margie made last week."

I sit down at the computer and open up the graphics software I'd asked Taft to subscribe to when I began my internship. And I start pulling in the new photos.

Alexis did a good job with the shots. They're well lit on pale-colored wood backgrounds. Very springy. So I begin experimenting with lighthearted graphic embellishments to try to produce a string of posts for a week's worth of content.

I'm a little tired, though, so I don't even notice Alexis behind me until she claps her hands together and startles me so badly the computer mouse flies off the edge of the desk.

"Oh my word!" Alexis hoots. "I apologize."

"No, it's fine," I say, clamping a hand over my suddenly pounding heart. "I just didn't hear you."

"That's good work, Abbi." She pulls out a chair and sits beside me. "I really like your content. It's so fresh."

"Thanks. I didn't use the photo of the slippers, though." I flip the screen to show her the picture that I mean. "The colors don't really pop here, and I didn't want to make the product look murky."

"It *is* murky," Alexis grumbles. "Those are stodgy, and no photo filter could fix it. All our slippers have that elderly look." She wrinkles up her cute nose.

"Tell us how you really feel," her father says from across the room.

"Dad, you know I'm right. We need some new looks."

"Felted wool slippers are in," I point out. "I think they'd fit the vibe without being too edgy."

Alexis blinks. "I was just thinking about those, too."

"Yeah?" I tap the computer screen, where I've got a photo of a plaid blanket enlarged. "I can see them paired with patterns like this."

"Good eye, Abbi," she says thoughtfully. "Tell me this—would a millennial wear felted wool slippers?"

"This one would," I say with a shrug.

"Interesting." She taps her lip. "Interesting."

TWENTY-SEVEN

A LOVERS' QUARREL WITHOUT LOVERS

Weston

Abbi is late for dinner.

She texted to say she was running late, so it's all good. But I find myself bouncing in my chair at the pizza place, watching the door for her.

Sometimes a guy just gets hyper. And tonight's my night. There's a lot riding on these two games against Merrimack. They're the only league team left that we haven't played. We'll play them back to back, two nights in a row. And if we were to lose *both* games, our playoffs spot is endangered.

So we can't let that happen.

Obviously.

Furthermore, my dad and my siblings finally drove up for a game. Not to mention Abbi's appearance—her first game of the season. This is why I'm practically levitating in my chair, waiting for Abbi to walk through that door.

"Maybe she's with her real boyfriend." Stevie snickers.

"Oh shut it," I grumble. The idea of Abbi finding a real boyfriend irritates me so much. It shouldn't. But it does.

I can't stop glancing at the door. Every time someone comes through it, I stare. "She's just running a few minutes late," I insist, because it's true. "We're supposed to go ahead and order. She'll eat anything, but she picks off mushrooms."

"Noted," Stevie says. And when he flags down a waiter, he orders three different pizzas.

"Three? For five people?" my sister argues. They bicker about it some more while I watch the door.

But it isn't until the pizzas are actually being delivered to our table that Abbi finally appears. I haven't seen her in a few days, but it feels like forever, so I drink her in. Her hair shines in the lamplight. She's wearing a dress and—fuck me —lipstick.

Which makes me focus on her mouth. And all the places on my body where I'd like to see it.

Now I might not survive this meal with my family. I'm thinking about sex instead of pizza or hockey, which is unfortunate because my near-term plans include only those last two things and not the first one.

Abbi spots me, probably because I'm shooting her a hungry gaze. Her eyes find mine. And then she walks bravely toward the family who made Christmas so very awkward.

"There you are, baby!" I pop out of my chair as she approaches. "Save me from these crazy people."

She gives me a shy smile as I pull her in for a hug. She smells like cold air and sweet perfume. "I dig the dress, but you didn't need to dress up for a hockey game."

"Hey, look!" my father crows. "It's the new bag in action. You look very professional, Abbi. Makes a statement."

"Thank you," she says, her smile warming up. "And I'm sorry I'm late, but I didn't wear this dress for you, Weston."

"Oooh, burn!" Stevie chuckles.

"I was actually interviewing for a job."

"No way!" I say. "Where?"

"Let the girl sit down," Lauren complains. "What kind of a boyfriend are you?"

Stevie snickers again.

My sister is right, of course. But I give my brother a little punch in the arm anyway, and then I pull out Abbi's chair and plate up two slices for her. "What would you like to drink?"

"Just the water," Abbi says, pointing at the glass already awaiting her. "Thank you."

"Now tell us about this potential job," my dad says as I hand Abbi the plate. "How did the interview go?"

"Really well," Abbi says. Then she gives me a nervous look that I don't really understand. "I mean—any job offer is good news at this point. Today I got two, actually. When it rains, it pours."

"*Yes!*" I'm so happy for her, because I know she's been stressed out about this. "Let's celebrate. What are the jobs?"

She chews a bite of pizza before answering. "Well, one of them is in New York. I got an offer from a mortgage bank."

"Mortgages are important," my dad says. "Everyone needs a house to live in."

"True," Abbi says, but she looks hesitant.

"Hang on," I hold up a hand. "Is that the place where the guy kept looking down your shirt?"

"Yeah," she says quietly.

My sister groans. "That doesn't sound like a great workplace. I've had managers like that. They never learn."

"Which managers?" my dad asks. "Who do I have to maim?"

"Easy, killer," Lauren says. "This was back in high school. The guy who owned that ice cream stand was kind of a creep."

"Damn, Lauren. How come you didn't say anything?"

She shrugs. "The tips were good, and I didn't want you

and Mom to make me quit. I stayed out of his way. But it only worked because the summer was short. If I were depending on that man to advance a career, it could have been ugly." My sister turns to Abbi. "Do you know anyone else who works there? Like, a friend you could ask about the manager?"

Abbi chews her lip, then shakes her head. "That job is in New York, though. If I hated it, I'd be in a good location to look around for something better."

"But you'd also have a pricey lease," Dad points out. "You might not feel like you could quit."

Abbi blows out a frustrated breath. "Yeah, I did think of that."

"What if we don't try to plan Abbi's life before at least feeding her pizza?" I suggest, reaching for her hand. It's surprisingly warm for someone who's just been outside.

She interlaces her fingers with mine and squeezes.

"What's the other job?" my sister asks, because nobody in this family knows when to shut up.

"That's, uh, something that came up unexpectedly." She slips her hand from mine and takes a big gulp from the water glass that's on the table in front of her.

"Unexpectedly?" Now my interest is piqued.

"I had this internship last semester," she says.

"At the flannel place," my dad offers. "Great slippers, by the way."

She flashes him a tiny smile. "That's the place. They asked me if I'd interview with the whole family today, for a permanent job. And we talked for two hours, which is why I'm so exhausted." She takes another gulp of water. "But it was a really good meeting, and they gave me an offer letter and everything. There's even a signing bonus."

"*Nice*," I say, because I don't want Abbi to work for a sexual harasser.

"No *way!*" my sister yelps. "That's amazing. You wouldn't have to move to New York."

"Right," she says, giving me a quick sideways glance. "But I still have a couple of resumes in various places. I haven't made up my mind yet. It's a tiny company, so it feels risky to me in other ways."

I take a big bite of pizza and chew. It's really good. But I feel unsettled all of a sudden.

Abbi might stay in Burlington. That idea is just starting to sink in when my sister pipes up again.

"Omigod! If you're still in Vermont, you can come to my wedding! This is great!"

Uh-oh. Fuck. I never even told Abbi the date of Lauren's wedding. And now I can feel her eyes on me. Her gaze is giving me a sunburn all of a sudden.

"She should come to the wedding either way," Dad says. "Nobody goes to the office Memorial Day weekend. Why isn't Abbi on the guest list, Weston?"

"We uh…" I swallow a bite and try to figure out what to say.

But Abbi finishes my sentence. "We thought I might be moving." She licks her lips nervously. "Like, frantically unpacking my new apartment before my job starts the following week."

"But not if you're staying in Burlington," Lauren points out. "Tell us about this job."

Abbi's face is suddenly flushed. "Well, the daughter of the founders wants to create a whole new business line for younger shoppers. But it's a big deal for them, so it would happen slowly. I'd spend the first year learning about their supply chain and working on logistics."

"That's fun," Stevie says.

"It does sound like fun," I grunt. So why haven't I heard

about this? Not even a single word?

Abbi puts down her slice of pizza and wipes her fingers on her napkin. "Excuse me a second." She gets up from the table and heads toward the back of the place, where the bathrooms are off a dark little corridor.

And even as my family watches me with curious eyes, I stand abruptly and follow her. "Abbi, wait," I say as I practically chase her across the big room and toward the bathrooms beyond.

She halts in the corridor and turns around. Even in the dim light, I can see her eyes are troubled. "What, Weston?"

"What the hell is going on here? You didn't tell me about that interview. And now it's already a job offer? But it's a big secret? You haven't been answering my texts."

"My week was crazy. The job was kind of sudden," she says. "And honestly? I thought you'd be weird about it. Kind of like you're being right now."

My head jerks back at this verbal slap. "I'm not being weird. I'm just asking you how your week was."

She licks her lips nervously. "You and I are supposed to be *fun*, right?"

"Right," I agree, but I feel like I've lost the thread.

"My life isn't always fun. Looking for a job has not been *any* fun. And you made it clear that we weren't part of each other's futures. It's the same reason I was never invited to your sister's wedding, I suppose?"

Oof. "It's true what you said. I never thought you would be in Vermont over Memorial Day weekend."

"Well, I might be. Sorry if that's an inconvenience."

"Abbi—"

"You should have seen your face when your sister brought up the wedding. And that I'd be in Burlington. It wasn't joyous, Weston."

201

"I was *surprised*."

"Me too," she says with a sigh. "But it shouldn't matter, right?" She waves a hand between the two of us. "This, whatever it is, can still reach its natural end point. Tell Lauren we broke up. You don't have to fake it anymore. Or do I have that wrong?"

"No," I say, but I feel so confused.

"Then why did you invite me tonight, anyway? If I'm past my expiration date?"

"I just wanted to see you. But, uh, I didn't think it through."

Her face falls. "Well, I *did* think it through. And I'm tired of faking it with your family. It was funny until I got to know them a little. It isn't funny anymore."

"Okay," I grunt, feeling like an asshole. But I don't even know what I'm agreeing to right now. "Sorry."

"Now go eat your pizza. I'll be out in a second." She disappears into the ladies' room.

I go back to the table feeling deeply conflicted. This is why I don't do relationships—I don't want to fight with anyone. And I'm terrible at it. Abbi made a lot of good points.

It's true what she said—I've been jerking her around. I didn't mean to. But somehow it happened.

When I slide back into my chair, everyone eyes me warily. "Did you fuck up?" Stevie asks gleefully.

"Possibly."

He shakes his head. "I used to think you guys weren't a real couple. But obviously you are. Can't have a lovers' quarrel without lovers."

I take a big bite of pizza and try to tell myself that I didn't just fuck everything up.

It doesn't work.

TWENTY-EIGHT

SOME BONEHEADED THING

Abbi

I stare at myself in the bathroom mirror as I wash my hands. I see flushed cheeks and tired eyes. I feel so *off* tonight. Like the world is too bright and too loud.

There was really no need for me to pick a fight with Weston. I don't know why I lit into him for being a little stunned that I have a job offer here in Burlington. For months I've been telling him that I wanted to move to Boston or New York.

But it's hard to ignore the inevitable. I know he doesn't want a real girlfriend. I hadn't expected to change his mind. So it was almost a relief to force the issue.

And—fine—it hurt to hear that I hadn't been invited to Lauren's wedding. It's coming up so soon. My life is happening in fast forward. Graduation is just weeks away. I'm supposed to take one of these jobs and sail into the future.

The future seems scary and lonely, even if I never say that out loud. Even if that's not Weston's fault.

"Hey, Abbi."

I swivel to see Lauren walking into the bathroom, and I'm so tired that it hurts my eyes to move them. "Hey."

"Congratulations on the job offers. Both of them."

"Thanks," I whisper.

"The Vermont one sounds better than the squicky mortgage banker."

"Maybe," I hedge. "It's risky. They're trying something new."

"But trying new things is important." She cocks a hip against the sink. "I know my brother freaked out a little. Weston isn't good at this stuff. But I think he's really into you."

I give a slow blink, because I am just not in the right head space to discuss this with his sister. I think she's wrong. But I don't know what to say to shut this awkward conversation down. "I'll keep that in mind."

She grins. "You already know how ugly things have been for my family. You saw it yourself. The next time Weston does some boneheaded thing, just remember that he's gun-shy."

"I'll try," I say. "Thanks."

Then I leave the bathroom and go back to the table. Weston pulls my chair out for me as I arrive. He even gives me a tentative smile. Like he realizes our snit is stupid, and he's sorry.

He's so damn polite. He's such a good guy.

But he's not *my* good guy. And I'd better remember that.

Weston is the first to leave the restaurant, because he's required to arrive at the arena ninety minutes before the game. He kisses me on the cheek and I wish him good luck.

"Come out to the ice cream place with us, Abbi," Mr. Griggs says. "We can all walk over to the game together."

"I thought I'd run home and change before the game, and

leave my favorite designer bag at home," I say instead. "Maybe I'll see you there?"

"We'll save you a seat," Lauren assures me.

Leaving them behind, I head home. The February chill slices through me as I walk uphill toward my apartment. Inside, my place is freezing. So I wet the cloth and toss it up onto the thermometer valve again. It's time to put on a pair of jeans and my *Griggs* sweatshirt for the game.

But I just don't feel like it. My head is achy, and my throat is scratchy. Instead, I make a cup of mint tea and climb into bed wearing Vermont Tartan pajamas.

I honestly don't know what to do about this sudden job offer. They want to pay me a real salary that's about eighty percent as much as the New York job. With benefits, too. Burlington is cheaper than New York. I could move into a nicer apartment here on a smaller paycheck than I could ever afford in New York.

So it's a great offer, but I'm still unsettled. I hadn't pictured my future here in Vermont. I thought I'd escape to a city and start over from scratch. But that's proving harder than I thought, when every day already feels like starting over from scratch.

Is it a sign of weakness that I'd rather walk into the tiny flannel company every day and see the faces of people who appreciate me? Does that make me smart, or does it mean I'm not ambitious?

I sip my tea, hoping the hot liquid can make me feel less confused. Less shaky and sad.

As the start time of the hockey game inches closer, I just can't make myself get up and go to the game. Thinking about Weston makes my heart ache. He told me he's not a relationship guy. He's always been up front about that. The problem is that I'm not capable of keeping up our fling without wishing for more. Does that make me a cliché? The clingy girl who agrees to be casual and secretly pines to be the one who changed his mind?

How did I let this happen?

I watch the clock. My eyes feel dry and achy. I must be overtired as well as overwhelmed. I've got too much on my plate.

Maybe it would be better to end things with Weston right now, on my own terms. At least without him at the forefront of my mind, I can make my job decision with cool, calculated logic. It will be my decision alone. As it always should have been.

Soon the clock tells me that it's ten minutes until the puck drops. So I pick up my phone and begin to compose a breakup text.

Then I delete it. A text is too impersonal. I'll leave him a voice message instead.

My heart thuds with tension as I tap the microphone. "Weston, I'm sorry to snap at you tonight, but I made a decision." As I pause to choose my words, I feel the first hit of grief. "We should just stop seeing each other now, before it gets too strained. I've had more fun with you than I've had in years, no lie. But there are things I have to focus on now that aren't super fun. So I'm going to make the difficult choice to do that. There's no point to drawing out the inevitable. Be well and have a great time in the playoffs."

My throat seems to be closing up, so I'll have to leave it there. I tap the stop button and send the message before I lose my nerve.

And, yup, I'm already sad. When I scroll up, I see the lengthy string of cheery texts between Weston and me.

And I just ended it. Forever.

Ow.

I force myself to lock my phone and set it down on the nightstand. Weston won't get that message for hours. He's busy with his team. I can picture him in his hockey gear, his bright eyes flashing as he concentrates on the game.

Now I know the warmth of that gaze when its full power is focused on me. It's more potent than I ever would have guessed. And I'll feel so chilly when it's gone.

But what was the alternative? A few more weeks of his loving touch, followed by an awkward parting?

It's better this way. A clean break.

I slip down into the bed and sigh. Someday I'll look back on this time with joy, though. I'll remember when Weston got me to sing with him in the car on the way to Thanksgiving dinner. And I'll remember those gorilla noises he made as he tried to show me how to ski.

I'll have those memories and they'll make me smile, without this terrible ache I feel right now, smack in the center of my chest.

That might be a while, though.

Grief takes time. If anyone should know, it's me.

TWENTY-NINE

BECAUSE I WANTED TO SEE YOU

Weston

It's a great game tonight. Our first line is on fire. And on defense, Tate and I make total nuisances of ourselves, keeping Merrimack away from the crease and holding them to a single goal all night.

My guys put up four goals. It's the best kind of drubbing, and the hometown crowd is a sea of green sweatshirts and cheering. My family is right behind the bench, and Lauren even bought a pennant somewhere. She's waving and smiling whenever I return to the bench.

I don't spot Abbi. But I sure hope she's enjoying herself. And, sue me, I'm hoping she got a little thrill when I stripped the Merrimack sniper during my last shift. I'm too cool to brag about my exploits, but if she happened to witness that, then I'm a happy man.

So I'm feeling pretty great as the boys blast some music in the locker room after the game. And that good feeling lasts about a half hour, until I pick up my phone and find Abbi's message.

My hair is still wet from the shower as I'm listening to her tell me *we should stop seeing each other now*.

Immediately the glow of victory is extinguished. I'm not even sure she attended the game. I looked for her, too. I found my family in the stands, but I couldn't find Abbi.

And she's not coming over tonight.

Or ever again.

Fuck.

So this is what it feels like to be at the wrong end of a breakup. I hate it so much. It's not because it's a blow to my ego, either. I'm going to miss her. A lot. Even though I know Abbi is right. Even if I feel low after listening to her message.

We weren't ever supposed to become a real couple, although it was starting to feel like we were. Tonight she'd asked why I invited her to have pizza with my family. And the answer was so easy—*because I wanted to see you*.

But that isn't fair, is it? That was abundantly clear when my sister started spouting off about the wedding. The one I never invited Abbi to.

Note to self—the fake boyfriend thing is only fun until one or both of you forgets that it's fake. And who knew I'd be the one to forget?

Abbi didn't. She cut me loose, and I ought to be grateful.

So why do I feel so blue?

"Yo, Griggs," Tate says. "Whatcha doing standing there? Let's go play some Beer Jenga and get our drink on."

"*One* beer," Coach says from across the room. "Don't celebrate yet. Gotta beat 'em again tomorrow night, boys. And what the fuck is Beer Jenga?" Coach asks. "Wait—never mind. I don't wanna know."

"Right, Coach," Tate agrees. "Good call." He grabs me by the elbow. "Let's party."

I follow him out the door. But I don't feel like partying.

The next couple of days are rough. My brain goes in circles, like a dog chasing its tail. I vacillate between knowing this break with Abbi was inevitable, and a guts-deep feeling that I've just made a huge mistake.

Either way, it feels wrong to me to end things on a bad note. So I try to call her. Twice. But she won't pick up.

Then I try texting. *Hey, I know you're a little mad at me, and you made a few good points. But can we at least have a talk?* But I get no response.

And now I'm just plain irritated.

"How bad was this argument?" Tate asks as I sit on the bench in the locker room, checking my texts for the millionth time.

"It wasn't that bad! I had no idea Abbi was so damn stubborn."

"Then maybe it's better that you broke up," Patrick suggests.

"Maybe," I grunt. "But I'm in such a pissy mood. I feel so..."

"Dismissed," Paxton, Patrick's twin, says. "Prolly the same way the girls usually feel when you're done with them."

"No way," I argue. "They know the score going in."

"Do they?" Paxton mutters.

My shoulders slump. It's starting to dawn on me that I have inconvenient feelings for Abbi. If it weren't true, I wouldn't care so much that she's done with me.

Shit. How did this happen?

"Time for dinner," Tate says. "Let's go to the Biscuit."

I let out a low moan, and the whole locker room laughs.

"Aw, Griggs!" Tate says, patting my back. "Maybe this is just what you need. Your girl can't ignore you face-to-face."

I'm sure he's right. And I really want to talk to Abbi. But I'd rather do it without an audience.

"Come on, man." Patrick slaps my shoulder. "Back on the horse. Maybe you can find another playmate for the night. Someone to take your mind off her."

"That's not happening," I snap. Not only am I not in the mood, I'd never do that to Abbi.

"He's right." Tate says. "Our guy has to be discreet at the Biscuit after this. What if we lose our table?"

"What if the entire waitstaff turns on us?" someone else asks.

"Then no more wings and beer," Patrick says sadly. "Didn't we warn you about this already?"

"I'm not ready to switch to a steady diet of pizza," someone complains.

"Fix this, Weston," Tate says. "Do it for the team."

"Okay, guys," I sigh. "Let's go to the Biscuit."

I feel tense as we walk through the door. And part of me expects to see the lacrosse team newly installed at table seventeen, gloating while we try to find adjacent booths in the dining room.

But, no, our table is waiting. I take my usual seat and look around. Maybe Abbi will emerge from the kitchen and smile at me like she always does. Can't we at least stay friends? At least I'd have that.

But the minutes tick by with no sign of her. And it's that lazy manager, Kippy, who finally swings by to drop off waters and menus. As if anyone at table seventeen needs a menu. "Someone will be with you in just a couple of minutes," he says. "We're short-handed tonight."

That's when I feel the first twinge of concern. And it only gets worse when a harried Carly hurries up, pen and pad in hand, and works her way down the table scribbling down orders. But the whole time she's shooting me curious glances.

And when Carly reaches me, she doesn't ask for my order. "Where is Abbi?" she demands instead.

"What do you mean?" I fire back. "I was going to ask you the same thing. Abbi won't take my calls."

Carly blinks. "You're kidding. She won't take mine either. She didn't show up for work last night or tonight! And it's her one-year anniversary." She glances over her shoulder before continuing. "Kippy won't give her the bonus she's worked so hard for," she hisses. "He said she blew it by going AWOL. But Abbi would never *do* that."

My stomach bottoms out. What the hell happened to Abbi?

"I've been calling her every ten minutes for the past two hours," Carly says. "And she doesn't answer. I'm going to go knock on her door on my break."

But I'm already pulling on my coat. "Let me do it."

"What about dinner?" Paxton asks. "Should we put in your order?" I don't even bother to answer him. I'm already headed for the door.

But I pull up short as I pass the bar. That cretin Price is behind it, cutting limes into wedges. "Have you seen her?" I bark.

"Seen who?" he says with a snake-like smile.

"Abbi."

He makes a show of shrugging. "Thought you were the boyfriend. Isn't that your story? Aren't you sticking with it?"

I want to punch him in the throat, but I'm in too big a hurry. So I dart out of the restaurant and start hoofing it uphill toward Abbi's place.

Thought you were the boyfriend, Price said. *Aren't you sticking with it?*

I had been, if I'm honest. I'd stuck to it until two nights ago. And I'd been happy, too. Playing the part of Abbi's boyfriend—and then becoming Abbi's boyfriend—had suited me just fine.

Then I freaked out when she said she might stay in Burlington. And now it's hard to remember why. If something has happened to her, I will lose my shit.

I'll lose it at myself, I guess, because I'll be the one to blame.

I break into a run and make it to Abbi's front porch in record time. Her car is parked at the curb, which is a good sign, right? I lean on the buzzer to her apartment unit, and then I try the doorknob of the front door. It's usually open.

But nope. Not tonight.

Shit.

I buzz again, and I start pounding on the front door until I see someone descending the stairs. It's another college student, I think—a skinny guy with round glasses.

Stepping back, I try to look nonthreatening. Although he's eyeing me warily when he opens the door. "Hey man," I say. "My girlfriend didn't show up for work two days in a row, and I'm panicking. Can you let me knock on her door?"

"Uh…" he says, looking a little unsure.

"Or let me talk to your landlord? Abbi said the old lady lives on the first floor, and never turns up the heat."

"Well *that* is certainly true," the dude agrees with a snort. "Abbi is right here, no?" He points at the door just behind him.

"That's right, and I'm really worried about her."

He bites his lip. "Okay, come in."

I leap past him and knock on the wooden door to Abbi's

little studio. "Abbster, honey. Please open the door. I'm worried about you."

There is nothing but silence. I even press my ear to the door and hear nothing.

"Maybe she doesn't want to talk to you," the dude suggests.

"I can see why you'd suggest that," I agree. "But I'm telling you—something is wrong."

He sighs. Then he turns and heads down the little corridor toward the back of the building. A moment later I can hear him knocking on a door that's just out of view. There's a whispered conversation, and a tiny elderly woman with gray braids coiled on top of her head emerges with a huge number of keys on a giant ring. She's like something out of Dickens.

"Knock again, please," she warbles. "I don't make a habit of breaking in on my tenants."

I take a fist to Abbi's door and knock urgently. "Abbi, honey. We're worried about you. Open up."

Nothing.

"Step aside," Miss Havisham says, wielding one of her many keys. She unlocks the door and opens it slowly. "Oh dear," she says, and my heart plummets. "It's very cold in here. Like a refrigerator."

I lose all patience, pressing the door open further and sliding past the lady as fast as I move to evade an on-ice opponent. Abbi's room is dark, but I can make out a form in the bed. It's ice cold in here, and I stop breathing as I approach the too-still lump on the mattress.

"Abbi. *Honey*." I sit down and place a hand on the flannel of her pajamas. My heart is in my damn mouth until she shifts under my touch. "Hey beautiful," I say in a broken whisper. "What's the matter, sweetheart?"

"Sick," she rasps.

"Oh no," I croon.

"Hurts," she mumbles, curling more tightly in on herself. *Cold.*

I press the backs of my fingers to her forehead, which is burning up in spite of the chill in the room. "We're going to fix you right up," I say gently. "Everything is going to be okay."

It has to be.

THIRTY

YOU AND I ARE ALREADY BUDS

Abbi

When I'd said I never wanted Weston to leave me, it may have been a miscalculation.

Because he's *so* bossy. *Wake up, Abbi. Drink this, Abbi.*

Can't a girl get the flu in peace?

Not to mention that I probably look terrible—like someone who's been dipped in the fry basket at the Biscuit. Nobody wants the world's hottest hockey player wiping sweat off her forehead. Not if he's doing it only out of guilt.

Even if it feels really nice.

Especially when he kisses my forehead so gently afterward.

Damn it.

At one point I wake up and Dalton of all people is here. He's fussing with an ear thermometer and calling in a prescription. "Make sure she's getting fluids," he says to Weston.

"Yes. I will, sir."

And then we're back to *Drink this, Abbi,* and *Swallow this pill.* But I just want to sleep for a week.

Finally, I wake up again, and there's sunshine streaming in the window. That means it's late afternoon. It's quiet, too. Weston isn't sitting on the bed anymore, or fussing over me.

I roll over and groan into the silence.

"Oh, you're awake," says a strange voice.

"What the..." I sit up suddenly and the room spins.

"Easy," says a floppy-haired blond guy. He gets up from my sofa and approaches me slowly, on a set of crutches.

I squint, because he looks familiar. "You're a hockey player," I mumble. "What are you doing in my apartment?"

"Well, Weston had to go to practice. It's the playoffs, you know. But I couldn't go." He points to a cast on his leg. "So I'm here to make sure you're okay."

"I'm okay," I slur, falling back onto the pillow. "You can go."

"No way. I'm on duty."

"What?" My throat is sandpaper, and nothing makes sense. "What are you talking about?"

"Weston sent me to make sure you're okay. I'm supposed to message him every half hour. If I'm late, even by a minute, he blows up my phone."

"Um..." I try to swallow. "And how long have you been doing that?"

"Since noon."

"And it's...?" *Please say twelve thirty.*

"Four p.m."

"You've been watching me sleep?" I squeak. "I don't even know you. That's creepy."

"Nah, I'm Weston's teammate. Cooper. So you and I are already buds," he says, crutching past me on the way to my kitchen, opening my cabinet and locating the glasses on the first try. "You sound like you need a drink." He opens the fridge. "Ginger ale, fresh squeezed orange juice, Gatorade, or water?"

"What? I don't have any of those things."

He opens the door wider and shows me a full complement of beverages, plus a plethora of unfamiliar food items. "Weston stocked you up. After you have something to drink, you'll have your choice of soups, along with toast if you're feeling up to it."

I blink.

"So what will it be?"

I'm so confused right now. "I'd love some juice, I guess." But how is he going to carry it over here ? I start to get up but he grabs the juice bottle, shoves it into the big front pocket of his hoodie and closes the refrigerator before coming back to me.

"Thanks," I say, taking it from him. But then I can't get it open. My hands feel weak and ineffective as I tug at the lid. And I have the sudden urge to cry.

My unlikely caretaker sits down heavily at the edge of the bed, grabs the juice, and has it open with a quick turn of his wrist.

"Thank you," I squeak. Then I take a sip, and it's cold, sweet nirvana. Seriously, it's a miracle. Like I've never tasted juice before. I'm starved for it.

"There you go," he says. Then he pulls a phone out of a pocket of his shorts and points it at me.

"Whoa!" I shield my face with one arm while the other holds my precious bottle of juice. "Do *not* take my picture."

"But it's proof of life!" he insists, and I hear the shutter noise. "Maybe Weston will calm down if he sees you're conscious. Seriously, that guy was *freaked* that you were sick."

"Cooper!" I bark. "Do not send that to Weston."

He chuckles. Then he tosses his phone down. "Fine, fine. But Weston loves you. I don't see what's the big deal."

I let out a sigh. Of *course* he doesn't understand.

"Look—I've never seen Weston spend time with any girl but you. And I've *really* never seen him bolt out of the Biscuit like his ass was on fire like he did when he thought something happened to you."

"Why did he think that?" I ask cautiously. After getting feverish the night before last, I'd holed up at home, dosing myself on NyQuil.

"Carly said she was worried about you. Apparently you didn't turn up for work two nights in a row."

"Two nights in a..." Horror dawns inside me. "What day is it?"

"Tuesday."

My heart stops. "Oh my God."

"Yeah, you slept for three days."

"Oh my *GOD!*"

"You mentioned that."

"You don't understand!" I shriek. "I'm going to get fired. I won't get my bonus." The juice bottle wobbles in my hand.

He takes it from me. "Breathe, Abbi. They'll understand."

"They won't."

"How about some food?" Cooper's phone dings. He picks it up and reads a message. "Weston said practice is over. He'll be here in an hour."

"I need a shower."

Cooper frowns. "That's not on the list of things that Weston said you could have."

"Are you kidding me?" I sputter. "If I want a shower, I'll take a shower!"

"Sure, sure," he says, setting the juice bottle down and then heaving himself up. "I'll be over at your desk, facing the other way."

"You could just leave," I point out.

"No can do," he says, picking up his crutches again. "Weston wants me to stay, so I stay."

I let out a groan. I don't understand why Weston is calling the shots. He probably feels really guilty. I told him we should end things, and then I got the flu. It's just a coincidence, but the man took it personally for some reason. So I need a new plan.

Step one: Shower so I don't look like a leper.

Step two: Thank him for the juice and send him home.

Step three: Go straight to the Biscuit and beg Kippy for patience. Cry, if necessary.

It's not like I don't feel weepy when I think of my annual bonus snatched away from me.

Showering takes all my strength. After I manage to shampoo and dress in clean clothes, I want to curl up in a ball and sleep for another three days. But I won't let Weston see me look defeated. So I wrestle the sheets off the bed and stuff them into the hamper.

Remaking the bed feels like a marathon, though, and Cooper takes pity on me and helps.

"You don't have to do that," I say. "But you're awfully good at hospital corners."

He just shrugs. "Are you going to dry that hair? Weston will yell at me if he thinks you look cold."

"Oh for God's sake!" I hobble back into the bathroom and spend a few tiring minutes with the blow dryer. Then I brush my teeth. That done, I throw my clean self on the clean bed and moan, because my heart is pounding like I just ran a marathon.

"Aren't you the picture of health," Cooper says. "Maybe this will help?" He's inched his way toward me with a bowl of soup in one hand and a crutch under the other arm.

"You really don't have to wait on me," I say, grabbing the bowl as it wobbles. "That's dangerous."

"Yeah, because you look so competent yourself." He chuckles. "Eat the soup, Abbi. Why do you hate getting help?"

"I don't," I snap, but it's only half true. Help is wonderful. But you should never get too used to it. I look down at the bowl. It's full of steaming chicken noodle. "Thank you," I manage.

"Don't mention it." He pulls a spoon out of his pocket. "Mind if I have some, too? There's more."

"Of course not. Dig in."

"Just don't tell Weston," he says.

"I won't. Cross my heart."

The floppy-haired surfer boy gives me a smile and crutches back to my kitchen.

After we manage to get the dishes cleared, it's time to face another problem. I locate my phone on the floor under the bed, and warily unlock it.

I find a couple of missed calls from Weston, of course, and some text messages asking me to call him. But the most frantic messages on my phone are from Carly. *Where are you? What's wrong? Kippy is so mad! Call me.*

Oh boy. That can't be good.

I'm terrified to open my email. The first thing I spot is a polite message from Taft at Vermont Tartan, asking if I've had a

221

chance to make a decision about the job. Then there's a follow-up message explaining that he'd heard from Dalton that I was ill, and to take my time.

Then, in a complete study of contrasts, I find a pissed-off email from Kippy at the Biscuit. *Abbi, this is unacceptable. Two shifts blown without a phone call? We have terminated your employment. Your last check will be issued within 10 days.*

"Oh my God," I breathe. Then I let out a tortured groan.

That's when the door pops open and Weston enters carrying my keys. "What's the matter? Why is Abby moaning? Cooper, what have you *done?*"

"Calm down, Westie," I say, dropping my phone onto the bed. "I was groaning at an email."

Weston stalks over to me, setting my keys on the night stand, and sitting on the edge of the bed. His beautiful eyes find and hold my gaze. "Cooper, you're dismissed," he says without even a glance at his teammate.

"Yes, sir." Cooper chuckles. Then he rises, grabs his crutches and heads carefully toward the door.

"Thanks for the, um, help," I manage.

He flashes me a quick smile before he disappears.

Even after the door shuts, Weston continues to stare at me with clear, serious eyes. "How are you feeling?" he whispers, taking both my hands in his.

I don't know what to do with that penetrating gaze, and it rattles me. "I'm, uh, doing fine. Nothing to see here. Thanks."

Awkward much? Yikes.

Nonetheless, Weston leans in and gently kisses me on the forehead. His lips linger, and I stop breathing. "Don't think you're feverish anymore."

"Right. Yep."

Next, the soft brush of his kiss lands on my nose. And this

bit of tenderness makes my eyes feel hot, and my chest ache with a sudden pang of longing.

"Abbi," he says gently. "I'm sorry I was a dick."

"It's nothing," I insist. "I get it."

He shakes his head once. "No, I don't think you do. You mean a lot to me. I was afraid to say so before."

Oh boy. "Weston, I'm really fine. Don't feel bad for me. There's no tragedy here. Everybody gets sick."

"Yeah, but everybody isn't you." He swallows roughly, still gazing into my eyes. "I realized something this week, Abbi."

"What's that?" I ask, trying not to fidget. All this attention is uncomfortable for me. I know I'm pale and have bags under my eyes.

"I love you," he whispers.

Wait, what?

"I love you," he repeats. "And I'm sorry I had so much trouble admitting it. I tried really hard to keep things casual, but I failed. And when Carly told me you didn't show up for work, I finally understood how much I need you."

"Weston," I breathe. "I'm sorry for the drama. But just because you got worried for a minute doesn't mean you—" I almost can't even say it out loud, because I want so badly for it to be true. "Love me."

"Oh, it does," he says with a bashful smile. "I'm the one who said we should just be friends who also have sex. But now I can't remember what that even means. When you're really close friends, and you also have really hot sex, that only adds up to one thing. At least for me, anyway. It means you're my person, Abbi. And I want to keep being friends and keep having gratuitous amounts of sex for years to come."

We're just staring at each other now, and I might be in shock. "Gratuitous amounts?" I repeat nonsensically.

"Well, yeah." Then Weston wiggles his eyebrows. Because he's Weston, and he's fun even when he's being serious.

A weird half-giggle escapes my throat before I choke it back. Then my eyes fill. "I could, um, get behind this idea."

"Could you please?" he whispers.

"Y-yes," I say shakily. Although I have to wonder if my fever has caused some kind of delirium. If I wake up and realize that Weston didn't actually just say all those wonderful things, I'm going to be inconsolable. But just in case this is actually happening, I'd better tell him how I feel. "I love you so much," I gasp. "I tried not to."

"Same, same." He smiles, and pulls me into his arms. I rest my cheek against his flannel shirt. "So this all worked out just like we planned, no?"

"No," I agree, and he laughs. I hear it in stereo as I burrow a little further into him.

"I fought it hard," he whispers, "because I didn't think I was good enough for you."

"What?" I yelp. "You're the best man I know."

He shrugs, then kisses the top of my head. "But you deserve the best, Abbi. I thought you deserved someone who wasn't all twisted up after watching his parents betray each other. I thought you needed a pro-level boyfriend."

"But you are," I insist.

"Nah. Those don't exist. There's only flawed guys who try hard. That's me. Just promise me one thing."

"What?"

"You'll come to my sister's wedding with me. If you're going to be my real girlfriend now, I need a date to this thing. And not just because you have a way with my dad. I'm in it for the arm candy." His smile is incandescent.

My heart flutters. "Sure," I say easily. "I'd love to come,

although I think your dad will be okay this time. And Weston?"

"Yeah?"

"Just for the record, I don't find either of your siblings the least bit attractive."

"Good to know," he says, rocking me against his sturdy chest. "Good to know."

THIRTY-ONE
ALL THAT GRATUITOUS SEX

Weston

Abbi is still pretty wiped out by the flu. "You probably shouldn't be this close to me," she says as I hold her tightly. "What about the playoffs?"

"I had a flu shot," I mumble, hoping that actually matters. "There's no way I can leave you alone right now. I miss you too much. Just deal with it."

"Yes, sir."

"That's more like it. Can you eat some more? We need to build you up."

"For all that gratuitous sex?" she asks.

"Exactly," I say gruffly. But it's a lie. I just want Abbi to be okay. "How about a frozen fruit bar? I got a box for you at the grocery store." Plus a hundred other things. That's what a distraught guy does when the woman he loves has a fever.

Abbi goes still. "You brought me frozen fruit bars?"

"Yeah, and then I had to jam the box into your tiny freezer. Please don't tell me you hate them."

She shakes her head slowly. "I love them. That's what my mother used to buy me when I had a fever."

Oh, man. See? This flawed, jaded guy really can do a thing or two right once in a while. "I think they're mixed berry. Want one?"

"Let's each have one."

I get up and fetch two bars, and I also put a movie on my laptop. We spend the evening curled up together. Abbi nods off from time to time, her soft hair tickling my chin. But I wouldn't trade this for anything.

When you love someone, reruns and fruit bars are all the fun you need in your life. It's more than enough.

The next night, though, I don't go over to her place after practice. After a grueling pre-playoffs practice, I send her a delivery of hot soup and a series of texts to make sure she's doing okay.

Totally fine here, Westie. Getting bored, though. I want to call Kippy and beg for my job back, but I think I should write a letter instead. Dalton says he'll give me a doctor's note.

A paper trail is a good idea, I reply. But the truth is that I have a few ideas of my own.

After practice, as we're all toweling off in the locker room, my teammates bring up the Biscuit as a matter of course. "You coming?" Tate asks, snapping his towel in my direction. "Maybe we should send Abbi some takeout."

"I got that covered already," I admit. "But I was planning on stopping by the Biscuit anyway. I need your help with something, guys. Listen up, okay?"

They gather around me, and I lay out my plan.

A half hour later, we're assembled around table seventeen, as usual. Carly—after inquiring about Abbi's progress—has dropped off glasses of water and reeled off the specials. But when she comes back to take our order, I ask to speak to the manager instead. "We have something to say to him. Can you let him know?"

She blinks. "Of course. Just don't get me fired."

"I would never."

Kippy arrives a couple of minutes later, his eyes shifting around the table, looking for problems. "What can I do for you gentlemen?"

"Well, we were doing some math earlier," I say. "According to my credit card bill, I've spent nine hundred dollars here in the last few months. And I'm not the only one. Guys?"

"I spent a thousand," Lex says.

"I spent seven hundred," Tate chimes in.

"I don't do math if I can help it," Patrick says. "But I get drunk more than most of these guys, so you better assume my bill is the highest."

"He spent twelve hundred and seventy-seven bucks, and I spent eight hundred," his twin says.

Around the table we go, as the numbers mount. Kippy holds up a hand to stop us. "Okay, I see the trend. What are you looking for? A free basket of fries? I could stomach some kind of unofficial rewards program, if you're quiet about it."

"No, man," I say, trying to keep the anger out of my voice. "This is not a shakedown. We were perfectly happy to spend our cash here—until you fired Abbi for getting the flu. By email, no less."

"That's *cold*," Tate adds.

Kippy frowns. "But she didn't even *call*."

"Yeah, that's how *sick* she was," I say, my hands in fists. "Didn't you stop for a second and wonder why your most reliable employee—tied with Carly here, who we also think is great—didn't show up? Wouldn't a decent boss *worry* a little if that happened?"

Kippy's nostrils flare, because I've just called him out for being an asshole. "I don't have time to babysit my staff."

"Sure," I say with a shrug. "But we don't have time to drink beer and eat wings here until you offer Abbi her job back. With the one-year bonus intact."

His ears redden as he glances around the table.

Eleven hockey players look back at him with solemn expressions. "We like pizza, too," Cooper says. "Pretty sure they could find room for us next door."

"And for our entourage, too," Patrick adds. "The hockey lovers of Burlington come to the Biscuit for us, you know."

I never knew Patrick's ego could be so useful, because Kippy blanches. Then he swallows hard. "Abbi can come and see me tomorrow," he says. "We'll work something out."

"That's not good enough," Tate chirps. "Call her right now. She's probably worried about her job. She's conscientious, sir. You don't let a good employee go."

Slowly, with a trapped look on his ugly face, Kippy reaches into his pocket for his phone.

"Here," I say cheerfully, handing him a Post-it note. "This is her number."

Scowling, he starts tapping it into his cell. Then he puts the phone to his ear. "Er, hello, this is Kippy at the Biscuit. How are you, uh, feeling?" he stammers, like it might kill him to care.

I guess that used to be me, though. I thought it would kill me to care too much for Abbi. Yet loving her is the best thing that ever happened to me.

"You, uh, can have your job back. And your bonus will be waiting for you. I'll write the check tonight."

He goes silent, listening to Abbi's response.

That's when I nod at Carly, who's beaming. "All right, let's do this order! I'll have the—"

"Thai spiced wings?" she guesses. "And a Coke?"

"Yup," I say, handing over my menu. Because some of my habits never change, and that's okay.

A few minutes later, I'm just taking my first sip of soda when my phone starts pinging with texts from Abbi.

OMG you will not BELIEVE what just happened!!!! Kippy called me. I got my job back, and my bonus!

That's great, baby, I reply.

In other news… I've decided to take the job at Vermont Tartan. Tell me how you really feel about me staying in Burlington. Be honest.

I feel great about it, I tap out quickly. *Less phone sex. More real sex.* I add a string of eggplant emojis because I'm classy like that.

Well that clears things up, she says.

Eat your soup. You're going to need the energy. What are you going to spend your bonus on?

The deposit for a new apartment. Somewhere with a full-size freezer, where you don't have to trick the heating system to stay warm.

I liked keeping you warm, I admit. *But I agree about your pad. Tell that landlady you're outtie.*

No more bad jobs or bad apartments. She agrees. *It's the end of an era.*

And the start of another, I add. Then I follow it with a bunch of heart emojis, because I'm turning into a big sap.

But I think I like it.

THIRTY-TWO

SHOOT!

Abbi

"Omigod. Omigod! SHOOT!" I scream as Weston rushes the net.

But he's blocked! There's a tussle, and Weston manages to keep the puck off the enemy's stick by firing it back to Tate.

I scream again.

Cooper laughs. He's seated on my left, eating popcorn and watching me freak out during the third period of Weston's game against Boston College.

On my right sits Carly. She has to go to work later. But this is a day game, so she can see the hockey team in action and then serve their supper afterward.

She won't, however, have to fend off Price while she does it. Carly told me earlier this week that my step-stepbrother has been fired from the Biscuit.

"I saw the whole thing go down, Abbi, and I'm sad there's no video. But he stole a bottle of premium vodka from behind the bar," she'd told me gleefully. "Then he put it in his pants on the way out. The new bouncer stopped him. He said—I swear to God—'*There's no way your dick is that big.*'"

I'd laughed so hard that Kippy gave me the stink eye. Not that I care much anymore about what that guy thinks. Now that my bonus check has cleared, I feel less pressure to take every shift he offers me. That's why I'm watching this hockey game with Carly on a Friday afternoon. I don't need to kiss Kippy's ass anymore.

Actually, I feel less pressure about *everything* except this hockey game. My semester will wind down in a few weeks. I'll graduate on the quad at the end of May. And then my full-time job will begin at the flannel factory.

My new apartment is already waiting for me, too. I'd started hunting while I was recovering from the flu. And I'd found a sunny renovated one-bedroom in a walk-up brick building off of Church Street. It was available immediately, however. So I called my landlady, who said she'd end my lease early if I wanted. "I finally got a buyer for this place," she'd said. "He can find his own tenants."

So that was an unexpected stroke of luck. My new place is sitting empty, though, until I move in there ten days from now. I can't wait.

From the new place, it will be a short walk to work in one direction. Or, in the other direction, I can walk uphill to meet Weston on campus. He's spending the summer in Burlington too. He's got a nine-to-five job working as a clerk in the hospital.

"To burnish my stellar resume before I apply to med school," he said. "But we can drive to my dad's lake house on the weekends. How do you feel about paddleboarding?"

"I'll learn," I'd told him, "especially if you'll make gorilla noises while you demonstrate."

"Nah. Dolphin sounds this time." Then he'd made the sound of a dolphin's snicker, and I'd laughed so hard I got the hiccups.

I'm really looking forward to the summer, and not just because I'll get to see Weston in a bathing suit. I've got so many things to look forward to—a new job. A new apartment. More time with Weston and Carly.

And I won't have to smell like Buffalo wings every night anymore. Those days are almost behind me.

But first we've got to win this game before I die of excitement. It's the third period, and the score is 3-3. There are eight minutes left on the clock, and it's a struggle not to leap out of my seat every time we touch the puck.

"Ooh, penalty," Cooper says.

"On who?" I scan the ice, full of anxiety. But then a BC player heads for the penalty box, and the announcer calls the penalty against him. "What's high sticking?" I ask my companions.

"I don't know, but it sounds wonderfully dirty," Carly says.

Cooper almost chokes on his soda. "I could demonstrate later."

"Nice try, freshman." She reaches over and takes his popcorn, helping herself to a handful before passing it back.

I decide I don't need to know what the penalty is for. I just need us to capitalize on this power play. "LET'S GO, WESTON! Put the biscuit in the basket! And I'm not talking about the restaurant!"

"He can't hear you," Carly says.

"You don't know that."

And Weston already told me how happy he was that I could attend this game. "Even if we don't make it any further than round two, I'm psyched you're coming," he'd said.

Now we have a power play, and I'm vibrating with excitement. The speed of play picks up the moment the puck is dropped. Moo U takes possession, and they begin a patient game of keep-away.

BC mobs their own net, of course. They need to avoid giving up a goal until they're full strength again.

There's sweat dripping off Weston's face as he and Tate pass the puck back and forth. Time ticks down, and I feel each elapsing second like a penance.

"They're so calm," Carly says. "I'd be freaking out."

"You gotta have patience," Cooper says. "Gotta wait until fate gives you that chance. Kinda like Abbi waited for Weston to get his head out of his ass."

"Aren't you deep?" Carly snorts.

"No, I'm smart."

I don't hear the rest of their bickering, because there's a flurry of activity down on the ice. Lex Vonne makes a fast pass to Weston, who wings it toward the net so fast my eyes can't keep up.

The goalie twitches, and I see the puck smack into his stick. But then I lose track of it until Cooper lets out a shocked gasp.

"What just happened?" I yell as the lamp lights.

"Rebound off the goalie, into the net!" She lets out a whoop of joy.

My heart leaps. "Omigod. Was that a goal for Weston?"

"Nah." Cooper laughs. "They'll credit the poor goalie and give Weston the assist."

I clap anyway. "We'll take it. I think Weston and the goalie just won the game together."

"Don't jinx it," Cooper says. "There's time on the clock."

But sometimes things just go right for a change. And a few minutes later, Weston's team has won the game.

It's funny how I've become one of those girls who stands around outside the locker room and waits for the team to come out. But here we are. The hallway is crowded with families and girlfriends and even some sports reporters. It's madness.

Eventually the players begin to emerge one by one, to loud cheers from everyone in the hallway. And when it's Weston's turn, the cheering is deafening. There are back slaps and fist bumps, and I wait patiently for the hullabaloo to die down.

But when our gazes finally lock, Weston smiles.

God, that smile.

"Abbi," he growls, weaving toward me. "Thank you for coming."

"Wouldn't miss it." He scoops me up and lifts me clear off my feet. I can smell the shower soap and feel the scrape of his whiskers against my face.

"God, it's crazy here." He chuckles, glancing around the hallway. "And I really want to get the hell out of here with you. But there's, uh, a quick press conference."

"Really?" I laugh. "So fancy."

"I know, right?" His grin is self-conscious. "Coach wants me there because of that crazy goal at the end."

"It *was* crazy," I say, dazzled by his blue eyes. "You take your time. But I'm going to hustle over to my new place, okay? Dalton wants to drop off my boxes before he leaves town for the weekend."

My stepfather has put three cartons of my mother's books in the trunk of his car, because my new apartment finally has enough room that I can shelve them. And because Lila wants them gone.

"I was going to carry those for you." His forehead wrinkles with concern. "Won't they be heavy?"

"Dalton will help me," I say, hugging Weston quickly. "Go and be important and come over when you're done."

"Okay." He gives me a single kiss, but there's a lot of expectation built into it. Weston is always fired up after a win.

We're going to have a *great* time tonight. I'm looking forward to it. "Did you know I'm having a new mattress delivered tonight, too?"

"Baby, I'm counting on it." He gives me one more scorching kiss before I peel myself out of his arms and make myself go.

———

Thirty minutes later I'm walking slowly around my new apartment. It even has that new place smell—fresh paint and optimism.

Night has fallen already outside my window. My footsteps echo against the wood floors of the empty living room as I wait for Dalton to show. I'm lucky that he's willing to stop here at six on a Friday before he starts his weekend.

You might find on-street parking, I text him. *But if you don't, I'll come down and get the boxes so you don't have to find a lot*.

And then I'll probably just stand there on the sidewalk with three heavy boxes and wait for Weston to rescue me. But that's not the end of the world.

Don't worry, Dalton replies. *My new assistant will carry them up*.

That's a lot to ask of an assistant, but I'm not going to complain.

Twenty minutes later, someone buzzes the door downstairs. I press the button to admit him. It might even be Weston. I'm not sure how long press conferences take.

Two minutes later, I hear someone slowly climbing the steps. So I block the door open to make this easier. "Over here! Thank you!" I cry as two of my boxes come into view.

But my heart drops as I get a better look at Dalton's new assistant.

"Fucking heavy," Price curses.

"Just put them down," I say quickly. "Doesn't matter where. I'll take care of it."

He squats down and I say a quick prayer that he won't strain his back—only because I know he'd blame me if he did.

"*Fuck*," he says again. Slowly he straightens up. "Not my job to haul your shit around, princess."

"Right," I agree nervously. "Thanks, though."

He takes a step closer to me. "You can do better than that."

"Better than…?" I take a step back. "Never mind. Go home, Price. Don't worry about me."

"I need a real thank-you," he says, his smile mean. "Show me some gratitude."

"You want a tip?" I snap. "Heard you aren't getting those anymore after you were fired from the Biscuit."

He makes an angry sound, and I instantly regret saying anything. How dumb am I? Now he's stalking toward me with fury in his eyes. "You stuck-up little bitch. Always gotta rub my nose in it."

"In what?" I babble, edging to the side. The door is still open. I just need to get past him.

"Fuck you," he sneers. Then he lunges.

I leap forward, almost getting clear of him. But he catches me by the wrist.

As soon as I feel his thick fingers close tightly around my arm, fear washes through me. Bile climbs up my throat. I've really done it now.

He shoves me against my clean white wall, both his hands on my arms. "Now I've got you where I want you."

"Where's D-Dalton?" I stammer. "He'll be w-waiting for you."

"Let 'im wait. I'm busy here." Price releases one of my arms, only to put his meaty hand around my throat.

It's not tight, but I've never been so scared. The threat is there. I open my mouth to scream, but I gag instead.

And he *laughs*.

That's what snaps me out of my inaction—anger. This fucker doesn't actually want me. He just wants to be terrifying. We're standing so close together that I don't have much room to move.

Still, it's enough. I lift one foot off the ground and knee him between the legs.

It's not a direct hit, but he still lets out a shout of surprise. "FUCK, Abbi. You fucking CUNT!"

I lift the other foot, preparing to try again, when I hear a crash in the doorway—the sound of a box of books being dropped too quickly onto a wood floor. "What the hell are you doing?"

Dalton. My God, I have never been so happy to see anyone in my life.

Price has already released me. "Nothing. Just fucking around."

This is the moment when I should start yelling. I should let both of these men know how bad it really is, and how I'm not going to take it anymore.

Instead, I put both my hands around my throat and start shaking like a paint mixer at the hardware store. A sob escapes from my throat.

"Oh God. Abbi," Dalton says in a hushed voice. "Oh God."

I sink slowly to the floor. I'm fine now, right? How come I can't even hold myself up?

"Hey guys!" Weston's voice says from the doorway, and I lift my head from my hands, like a seedling toward the sun. "Whoa. What the fuck is *he* doing here? Abbi?" Weston crosses the room in a flash, lowering himself to his knees in front of me. "Abbi, hey, what happened?"

I'm pulled against his chest in gentle arms, and I take my first real breath in ages.

"Get out," Dalton barks, presumably to Price. "Get out of my sight."

"Call the police," Weston says. "Not joking."

My apartment door slams, which is probably Price's doing. And a moment later Dalton is also kneeling on the floor in front of me. I let out a terrified sob, and it echoes in the empty room.

"Why didn't you tell me?" Dalton pleads.

"She *tried*," Weston says through clenched teeth. "You brushed her off."

I look up at Dalton, whose mouth is opening and closing like a fish. "She said he pestered her, but I never…" His mouth flops around some more.

The thing is, I don't know exactly what I said to Dalton. I don't remember the precise words I used. "It was him or me," I whisper, knowing that I'm not making a lot of sense right now.

"She thought you'd take your new wife's side," Weston says. "Can you really blame her? It's not like she has a lot of family to spare."

"*Shit.*" I don't even know if I've ever heard Dalton curse before now. "Abbi, I'm sorry. You should have—" He swallows. "I should have asked you more questions."

"You *know* he's a troll," I bite out. "Can't finish a sentence.

239

Can't hold down a job. So you just *hired* him after he got fired *again?*" My voice is shaking.

Dalton groans, scrubbing his face. "You're right. I don't know what to do about him. I don't have a damn clue. I was just trying to go easy on him for Lila."

"He doesn't need someone to go easy," Weston growls. "But I guess you know that now. That asshole kept Abbi on the run from her only *home.*"

"Jesus." Dalton goes pale. "Abbi, I'm so sorry."

"It's okay now," I croak. It's not like I want to move back in. "But I refuse to be around him again. Not even on Thanksgiving."

"Okay, okay." Dalton sits heavily on the wood floor, looking uncomfortable in his suit pants and white shirt. "Can I take you two to dinner? I feel terrible."

I *almost* say yes. It's on the tip of my tongue. But I don't want to go out with Dalton. I want a night just with my boyfriend. "That's a nice offer, but we have plans," I say quietly. Because I'm finished being the girl who works too hard to stay in Dalton's good graces.

I've got to stop being afraid to ask for what I need.

"All right," he says heavily. "I'll leave you two alone." He glances around the room. "Is it pushy of me to ask if you have plans to get some furniture? You said no when Lila asked you if you wanted to look in the attic."

"What if she said no because that meant dealing with Price?" Weston asks.

Dalton blanches. "Did you, Abbi?"

"Maybe," I admit. "Can we talk about it another time?"

"Of course," he says, rising to his feet and dusting himself off. "Please take care of yourself, and we'll talk soon."

"I will. Thank you."

Dalton lets himself out, and the sound of the door closing

echoes in my empty space. "Wow," Weston says. "There's some drama for your Friday. Are you okay? What did Price try, anyway?"

I lean back against the wall and close my eyes. "Intimidation," I mutter. "Humiliation. He pinned me against the wall just to be terrifying."

Weston makes a very unhappy noise, and I hope he's not plotting Price's murder right now. "What do you need?" he asks after a deep breath. "How can I make this better?"

"You know what?" I wipe my hands on my jeans and will my body to relax. "You already are. It's Friday night. My mattress isn't due to show up for..." I check the time on my phone. "Ninety minutes. I asked them for the latest time slot, because I didn't know if there was a team dinner you'd have to go to."

Weston shakes his head. "I'll see them tomorrow."

"Can we go sit down at a restaurant on Church Street? I just want to go out with you. I want to have *fun*." There's that word again, although it's growing on me. I haven't made enough time in my life for fun.

I could start now.

"That we can do." Weston gets to his feet, then holds out a hand to pull me up. "Let's see... Sushi? Ramen? Burgers? What are you in the mood for?"

"Just you," I whisper. "I don't care what we're eating. I just want to have dinner with you."

Weston stops in front of the door and turns around. His smile is tender as he pulls me into his arms. "That's easy, isn't it?"

"Yes," I agree as he gives my cheekbone a slow kiss. "I'm easy to please."

"You know what else is easy?" he asks, kissing the corner of my mouth.

"What?" I brush my knuckles against his evening stubble.

"Me," he says, nipping my ear. "I'm easy. And I will show you how easy about fifteen minutes after that mattress shows up."

"Will you, now?"

"Bet on it, girl. Bet on it."

THIRTY-THREE

EPILOGUE: TOTALLY WORTH IT

Weston

"Westie, what room are we sleeping in?" Abbi asks as we drive through the back roads of Fairlee toward my father's house.

"Oh baby, we're taking that double bed again. Stevie and Tamar can take the bunk room."

"Hmm. Are they down with this plan?"

I shrug. "Doesn't matter if we get there first."

"Devious, Griggs. I like it. I don't know if we can make sex noises this time, though."

"What?" I gasp. "It's a tradition. Besides, they'd be *real* sex noises." I nudge her with my elbow, because I'm subtle like that.

"No way," she says. "I have to be able to look your brother and Tamar in the eye over the turkey tomorrow."

"You're forgetting something, though. Stevie and Tamar might be making their own sex noises. They won't even hear us."

Abbi thinks this over. "Maybe if we're *very* quiet."

"Uh-huh," I agree. The old bed squeaks like a piglet on

cocaine, but I'm too smart a man to point that out right now. "Five more minutes until we get there," I say instead. "Just enough time for a singalong. Cue up the Avett Brothers?"

Abbi claps her hands. "'Ain't No Man!' Yes! Another tradition." She taps furiously on her phone, and a few seconds later the intro kicks in, and then we start to sing.

I actually slow down the car so that we won't arrive before the song is over. We really go for it, too, singing loud through the chorus and into the verse.

Tomorrow is Thanksgiving Day, but this year I didn't hang up my sign to advertise for a date. I already have the perfect date.

Although we're not on our way to Dalton's house this year. And I'm no longer avoiding family holidays. This year we're headed to my dad's. And this way Dalton can host Price—who no longer lives in his home—and keep peace with his wife.

Dalton had asked Abbi first, though. He'd extended an invitation, explicitly stating that if we wanted to join him for Thanksgiving, that Price would not be included. Dalton and Lila have finally figured out how "tough love" for that asshole works, but I hear that it wasn't easy.

The Price situation actually sent Dalton and Lila to marriage counseling for a little while, until Lila learned how not to be her son's enabler. But I guess things are better now.

Abbi gently turned down Dalton's Thanksgiving invitation, though, telling him we were already spoken for. And so Dalton is taking us out to dinner on Sunday night, "just to catch up," he'd said.

Dalton and Abbi are in a good place lately. And neither of us needs a fake boyfriend or girlfriend anymore. We're just in it for the turkey and the stuffing this time. And Aunt Mercedes's cheesy mashed potatoes. And whatever pies my father bought from the bakery, because that man doesn't often cook.

I love Thanksgiving. Always have. But I love it even harder today, with my best girl singing her lungs out in the passenger seat beside me.

Even the car is different this time. Three months ago we traded in Abbi's heap of a car for a used Subaru Outback.

Yup, we bought a car together, which is a pretty big commitment. But next year—if everything goes according to plan—we'll probably live together, too. I'll be in medical school, and moving out of the hockey house. She'll be working her way toward world domination in the flannel industry. Sharing an apartment just makes sense.

I honestly can't wait. We spend most of our nights together anyway.

The final chords of the song resonate as I turn into the driveway and park behind my dad's car.

"Whew!" Abbi collapses against the seat. "That was a good one."

"The best," I agree, killing the engine. There's no snow on the ground yet, and the lake shimmers between the distant trees. Abbi and I came to stay here a few times over the summer. We had some fun swimming in the lake and roasting marshmallows in Dad's fire pit.

And I made gorilla noises on the paddleboard, just for old time's sake.

Abbi removes her seat belt, but I grab her hand before she can climb out of the car. "Happy anniversary, baby."

She turns to me with wide eyes. "It's sort of true, right?"

"You know it." I lean over and kiss her quickly. "I'll never forget knocking on your door on Thanksgiving last year. When you opened it, I was so surprised to find out that the hot waitress from the Biscuit was my date."

She rolls her eyes, like I'm humoring her.

"Believe it, girl. I totally wanted to take you home that night, too. Remember how I said we should save the other bottle of wine for later?" I wiggle my eyebrows.

Her smile widens. "I do remember. And then it didn't happen."

"Oh it *happened*, honey. Just not that night. We had some issues to work through."

"We did," she agrees.

I swivel around and reach into the back seat for something I stashed back there in secret. "Happy anniversary, honey." I hand her a wrapped present, which I'm sure she can guess is a wine bottle. "We'll have to chill this so we can drink it later."

"Oh! Who's a fun guy?" She rips the paper away and pulls out a bottle of champagne. But I've covered the label, with my own hand-lettered version. In brightly colored Sharpie it says: A BOTTLE FOR LATER. BUT NOT TOO MUCH LATER. BECAUSE I'M A MAN WITH NEEDS.

Abbi lets out a snort of laughter. "Subtle, Westie."

"I know, right?"

She gives me a kiss on the jaw. Then she pulls something out of her purse—a greeting card, with WESTIE on the enve-lope, and a drawing of a West Highland Terrier. "This is for you."

"Aw! Thanks." I slit the envelope with my thumb and pull out the card. On the front there's a cat in a turkey costume. Inside, I find twenty-five dollars in cash. And Abbi has written only: TOTALLY WORTH IT.

"Oh baby!" I say, laughing. "I love you so much. You're hilarious." Then I have to kiss her.

And we're still there, entangled in each other, until my dad taps on the window. "Did you know you're steaming up the car?" he yells through the glass.

Abbi, embarrassed, quickly opens her door and climbs out.

When I follow her a moment later, my dad is laughing at us. "You know, your brother used to have this dumb idea that you two were only pretending to date."

"Is that so?" I ask, unbothered, while Abbi makes herself very busy pulling her duffel bag out of the back.

"Yeah." Dad shakes his head. "Love that kid, but sometimes he's a dingus."

"Total dingus, I agree."

Abbi gives me a wide-eyed stare. And I just wink back at her.

THE
END

ALSO BY SARINA BOWEN

Moonlighter (Eric Bayer's book)

Loverboy

THE IVY YEARS

The Year We Fell Down #1

The Year We Hid Away #2

The Understatement of the Year #3

The Shameless Hour #4

The Fifteenth Minute #5

Extra Credit #6

GRAVITY

Coming In From the Cold #1

Falling From the Sky #2

Shooting for the Stars #3

HELLO GOODBYE

Goodbye Paradise

Hello Forever

CPSIA information can be obtained
at www.ICGtesting.com
Printed in the USA
LVHW100142251121
704426LV00007B/870

9 781950 155286